S.E Foster

Obsession

First publication: September 2015

S.E Foster

www.samanthaharringtonauthor.wordpress.com

This book is a work fiction. The names, characters, places, and incidents are products of the writer's imagination or have been used fictitiously are not to be construed as real. Any resemblance to persons, living or dead, actual events, locale or organisations is entirely coincidental. The author does not have any control over and does not assume responsibility for third party websites or their content.

Printed in the United States of America

First Printing, 2015

For my children - never give up. Always give it 110%, and know that I am proud of you all. You bring so much joy and love to my life. Never forget that, even when my head is in my laptop, I love you with all of my heart.

For my husband - for all the times you have pushed me to try when all I wanted was to stop.

You have cooked, cleaned and done the school run, then put all of our children to bed so I could stay up and write. Your support has never wavered through the good and the bad, the ups and downs.

For Mum and Dad who taught me about life and love, who always told me to work hard and never give up - without you both I would not be where I am today.

For my best friend, Charlie, your constant reading and the truth you tell me, for the times when I think I can't go on and write one more word, you are there every step of the way. You're always there whenever I need you, on the phone or in person. What more could a girl want in a friend?

This book would not be possible without your love and support. xxx

PROLOGUE

THE SMELL IS different when I wake, it's putrid. I cover my nose with my hand to stop the bile that rises in my throat.

I look around and I can see that I'm not in my room; wherever I am is cold and devoid of furniture. I can barely see my surroundings in the dim light. In the sparse room is the bed that I am sat on, a bucket in the corner and a chair; the door is on the other side of the small room. Gingerly, I start to get out of the bed placing my bare feet on the cold stone floor. The room is dark with only a small window which doesn't give off much light and the walls are really dirty. I make my way slowly over to the door, as I attempt to turn the handle I realise that the door is locked.

Sitting back down on the bed, I try to think about how I got wherever here is.

Me and my friends had just finished our final exams and had decided to go out and have a laugh and a few drinks, guilt free now that exams are done with, no more late nights in the library studying, up at all hours writing essays. What I never expected that night was to be taken.

The arm that wrapped around my waist, the hand that clamped around my mouth. I didn't feel his skin, just a cloth of some kind cover my mouth and nose. I tried screaming but it was no use, the world was fading. My last thought was of my family and friends, that feeling that I won't ever see them again or tell them I love them.

I start to cry recalling the events that led me to be here, the tears slide down my cheeks, my chest is heavy with panic. Why me?

I hear the click of the lock, the handle starts to turn, I push myself as close to the wall as I can get, huddling in the corner as I wait for someone to enter. I can feel the panic start to rise, I don't like this feeling of shear panic that is consuming me right now. I wait for whoever is going to come into the room my heart is racing, I feel my eyes burn as the tears threaten to fall again. The door opens and I can see the outline of a mountain of a man. He's tall and broad, his shoulders look like they could carry the weight of the world. He steps towards me and my breaths become shallow and rapid. As he gets closer I take in more details, like the stubble that graces his face, the way his black t-shirt defines the power of his muscles. He looks like the villain in every story I've ever read, all in black with his cargo pants and heavy boots.

"Here you go," he says to me walking over to the bed, I hadn't seen the tray he was carrying, he places it on the bed. His voice rumbles through me, its deep and sensual, I swear I feel it coat my skin.

"Where am I? What do you want with me?" I hurl the questions at him not expecting an answer.

"It's not you that we want Faith. You won't be hurt as long as you behave yourself and don't try anything stupid." He watches me as it dawns on me that he knows my name.

"How do you know my name?" I don't know where the steel in my voice comes from, I really hope it stays. "Who is it that you do want then?"

He turns back towards the door, but hesitates before leaving and turns back to me. "We know everything about you Faith, and it's your father that we want. He owes us money, and if he doesn't pay, well, then Faith, then you're his payment."

He walks out, closing and locking the door behind him, leaving me in my new cell.

My father is a business man. He wouldn't owe money, he invests it. Well, as far as I know, but then, in my 24 years I've seen more of my boarding school than I have of my father.

I look down at the tray on the bed, there's a bottle of water and a sandwich on a plate with a slice of apple. I'm so hungry that I don't care if it's days old . I tuck in and eat every last crumb, sipping the water to make it last. I don't really relish the idea of peeing in a bucket.

I drift off to sleep hoping that this is just a misunderstanding and that I will be home as soon as possible.

The next few days are pretty much the same routine. Nothingness until they take me to a bathroom to have a wash, and give me clean clothes to wear. Considering that I'm being held against my will, I'm not being mistreated. I am extremely grateful for this, though I think that's more down to Damien than anything to do with me. Damien is the guard who mainly looks after me. I think he's the head honcho because everyone answers to him and no one does anything without his say so.

Damien comes into the room I've dubbed my cell. "Your father has declined to pay what he owes. He's fully aware that we have you, and thinks that you are an exceptional payment to cover his debt."

"WHAT THE FUCK! YOU CAN'T DO THIS TO ME." I scream at him, jump off the bed and start pounding on his chest, tears streaming down my face; in this moment I realize that my dad does not love or care about me. I sag against Damien; his arms come around me holding me close to him.

"Shh, I won't let anybody hurt you Faith," he whispers into my ear.

I start to calm down, "What's going to happen to me?" I whispered into his chest.

"Nothing bad will happen to you Faith, I'll get you out of here, I swear." his words were said lovingly to me as if he really did care. "Just bide your time for now while I come up with a plan to get us out of here."

He places me on the bed, kisses the top of my head before leaving the room; I try not to dwell on the fact that he said us and kissed my head, but my tummy is a knotted mess.

All I know is that for now I'm still trapped in this room, and I can't do a damned thing about it.

Chapter One

Faith
Six months later

"FAITH, ARE YOU ready to talk about what happened?" I hear the therapists question, it's the same question she's asked every week since I started coming here. In the last 6 months my life has changed so much, and the only person that knows what really happened is my best friend Cami.

She has held me when I cried and comforted me when I woke in the night screaming, but most of all, she has given me somewhere to feel safe, somewhere to call home.

Am I ready to talk? I think today, maybe I am, maybe I can let some of it go. "Maybe" I mumble. She sits in her chair opposite me with her trademark pen and note pad.

"Whatever you're going to say Faith, it stays in this room." I have to admit her soothing voice does make me want to talk to her.

"I think I'm in love with Damien" I whisper into my hand not wanting to vocalise my dirty little secret. It's the first time that I have said it out loud.

"Who's Damien?" she asks me.

I don't know if I'm ready to tell her that yet. My head hurts with the commotion that is my mind.

Only Cami knows. She's safe, I can talk to Cami. I know that she will always listen to me without any judgement – but even she doesn't know I am in love with Damien.

"Damien, he's the one that got me out." I tell Dr. Smith. She's an older lady, slight greying at the temples with hair pulled into a perfect bun, but she has a soft kind face.

"How did he do that?" With her question I slip down the slope, back into the nightmare that plays on repeat inside of my mind. No longer thinking of Damien, but of the darkness. Of *Him*, and my cell. It was the darkest time of my short existence and I hate everything about it, except that it gave me Damien.

I shake my head at Dr. Smith, I can't do it. I pull my legs to my chest and my arms around them. I spoke his name. Why did I do that? No-one other than Cami knows his name. Regret fills me as the darkness that eats away inside, the hate that threatens to consume me tears me up. I cling onto the pain, that's where my memories lie. That's how I keep him close to me. "Damien" I sign. I can't forget. Ever.

"Please… I can't. Just, no more," I speak through the sobs that threaten to overtake me, the words not sounding quite right.

"Ok Faith, that's fine. You did well. Now, let's book you in for next week." I nod my head in answer.

I take some tissues out of the holder so I can wipe the tears from my eyes. "Thank you for today Dr Smith, I'm trying, I swear I'm trying" *Though maybe not fully* I admit to myself.

"Only when you're ready Faith. I'm a patient old bat" she says, trying to make me laugh. I don't remember the last time I laughed…

Making our way back to the waiting room, I notice Cami looking worried. I guess I'm not fooling anyone with puffy eyes and a tear stained face.

"Faith, are you ok sweetie?" She comes straight up to me and wraps me in her arms. The tightness in my chest eases a little. I'm safe.

I love Cami, she has always been there for me, more so since he saved me; she's my rock.

"I'm ok," I whisper to her, "I actually spoke a little today." Her arms squeeze me tighter at my words. She pulls away from me, holding onto my arms looking me in the eye. "I am so proud of you Faith!" Her eyes hold that sense of understanding that she knows that it's time I let someone else in, and that if I keep taking those baby steps, hopefully one day, I will come out the other side.

We head out to the carpark and climb into Cami's black and red Mini Cooper, which Cami loves for driving around in London. Starting up the car, "Hey Faith, do you want to try and have lunch out today? Or do you want to just head home?"

"Home please Cami. I'll make us something." I feel bad, but I know that she understands that I can't cope in the outside world yet. I have created this little bubble that I am safe in, and I'm terrified to leave it. She has tried time after time to get me out. I know that one day I will have to pull up my big girl pants and join the real world again but for now, I just can't face it.

I'm in the kitchen at the sink, washing up after the chicken salad I made Cami and I for dinner. It wasn't much, just cooked chicken breast chopped up, lettuce, cucumber, new potatoes, and tomatoes in a bowl with a bit of olive oil. I put the last plate on the drainer, the washing up finally done. With the joys of cooking comes cleaning but it has to be done: it's the least I can do since Cami lets me stay with her rent free.

Out of the corner of my eye, I notice someone lurking in the alley at the back of the house. I feel the hairs on my neck stand up and I shudder.

When I lift my eyes to fully look out of the kitchen window, I can't see anyone. Remembering the doctors' advice about when I become anxious, I take a few big deep and slow breaths to try and calm my racing heart. I feel it start to ease; I was never like this before. I get myself so worked up sometimes that panic consumes me. I feel weak, pathetic and helpless.

Some days, I think I'm going mad. I see Damien everywhere I go. I know he's not really there. He dropped me off at the hospital and I haven't seen him since. His last words to me where "Don't go home," and with that he left me there on my own.

I'm still taking deep breaths when Cami comes into the kitchen, "Did it happen again Faith?" I can't form the words to reply so I just nod my head. She starts to rub the bottom of my back to distract me from my thoughts. I do the only thing I know that will help me - fake humour, I've come to rely on it. I think Cami understands that when I do it, I just can't talk about it yet.

"Wine time!" I say in a silly singsong voice, I head over to the fridge pulling the bottle of white wine from the shelf.

"I'll get the glasses," Cami says and I know she has understood. I'm in the mood to totally forget about today. I come back to the kitchen island and pour two big glasses. The kitchen is lovely, it has high gloss plum units and white granite worktops, with stainless steel appliances finish its ultra-modern look.

The kitchen opens into the dining room, the glass table and 12 white leather chairs are to die for. When Cami moved me in six months ago, I was awestruck at this room. It's perfect for entertaining, not that she has done any of that since I moved in. I feel like such a burden to Cami, she has stopped doing so much since I moved in here and I feel like I'm ruining her life. I know that's not the case but when someone you love puts her whole life on hold to help you, I guess it's to be expected. I honestly don't know what I'd do without her. She is beautiful inside and out, right down to her core she is pure and selfless.

We're sat giggling on the black and grey corner couch in the living room, reminiscing about our University days. I must admit all this laughing has helped me forget for a little while today, and for that little while at least, I felt like the old me.

I place my empty glass on the oak coffee table, "That's me for the night, I'm going to get a bath and then try and get my head down for the night." I get up from the couch and place a kiss on her cheek saying night as I walk towards the bathroom.

I slip into the water, it's so hot, but I love the way it feels. The water is soothing and warm wrapping itself around me, making me feel so much better. I hear the sound of my phone going off, but I am so relaxed that I figure I'll leave it check it when I am done. It can't be anything important anyway.

Knowing I have to move saddens me but I lather up the body wash, and get rid of the signs of the day, I can feel all of the stress and grime of the day being washed away. If only it were that simple. Ha!

I rinse myself off and wrap myself up in a towel from the heated towel rail. Padding across the tiled bathroom floor to the vanity I get ready for bed.

I go back into my bedroom to put my PJs on, so that I can fall asleep. In my dreams I get to see Damien, I get to hear him speak. I need to hear him. It's become my addiction - reliving my nightmare just so I can be with Damien one more time.

Once I'm dressed I notice my phone on the dresser, remembering that I heard it go off earlier on.

Looking down at my phone I see a text from a number I don't recognize;

UNKNOWN: You will pay for what you have done Faith. This is far from over! I'm coming for you.

The words send chills down my spine making me feel sick to my stomach. I hear a scream and realise it's me as my phone falls from my hands and bounces off of the floor.

"Faith. Faith!" I can hear Cami shouting my name but I can't answer. I am frozen. Oh God no, I thought it was over.

Dropping to the floor, I am on my knees crying; my hair is still wet from the bath. I feel Cami's arms come around me "Ssshhhh, ssshhhh, Faith what's happened? Are you ok?" She is stroking my wet hair and rocking me like a child, I start shaking my head frantically, still unable to form words. I reach for the phone and pass it to Cami.

I feel her breath hitch as she reads the words on the screen, "We need to call the Police Faith. I know you didn't when it happened before but we need to tell them now, we have to keep you safe!" Her words send fresh tears down my cheeks.

"OK" I manage to whisper. She leads me into the living room and places me on the couch, wrapping me in the throw that's always hung over the couch.

I ask Cami to make the call: I can't stop my fingers from shaking to dial the number. I hear the call as she never leaves my side still stroking my hair while talking to the Police.

The next twenty minutes seem to last a lifetime; I flinch when I hear the ring on the phone for the apartment. Cami answers and lets them in, when she's walking back into the living room, I notice there are two police officers that follow behind. She comes to sit by the side of me, placing her arm protectively around my waist keeping me close to her.

"Are you Faith Young?" the police officer asks me.

"Yes," I answer quietly. I lift my head, quickly looking at the two police officers.

"I am PC Cooper and this is my colleague PC McCabe," he says pointing towards the other officer.

"Can we have a look at your phone please Miss Young?" I reach towards the coffee table to get my phone, PC McCabe takes the phone from my hand and passes it across to PC Cooper to examine.

"Have you had anymore messages like this Miss Young?" He asks me.

"No, this is the only one," I reply.

"Could this be a hoax from somebody?"

"No, I don't think so."

He looks at me like he does not believe my answer but I know the truth, I know what my father caused, I know I was kidnapped, and I most certainly know Damien got me out.

"Look Miss Young, with just one message there really isn't much that we can do, is there anything you're not telling us?" He asks looking directly at me.

"Nothing else has happened."

I can't tell them. I can't get Damien in trouble.

"Well, if you think of anything else, please don't hesitate to get in touch by calling the station."

I nod. As they get ready to leave, Cami gets up to see them out of the apartment, I know I'm about to get an earful when she comes back into the living room.

"What the hell Faith! Why did you not tell them what really happened?" She glares at me while she is yelling.

"I couldn't do it Cami, I can't risk Damien. He got me out. I just can't do it to him." I plead with her to understand what I'm saying. She throws up her hands in exasperation.

"You need your head tested woman! He may have set you free in the end, but he still helped hold you in that godforsaken place."

I see the anger on her face, she is furious at me. I pluck up the courage to try and explain.

"If it wasn't for him Cami, I don't know what would have happened to me." My shoulders sag in relief when she finally nods her head, her mouth opens to speak but I cut her off. "I'm going to bed Cami, I really am sorry I couldn't tell them. I owe him something Cami, my silence is all I have to offer."

I check my phone again to see if there are any more messages, relief floods my body when I don't see any.

Pulling my covers back, I slowly climb into bed and cover myself up, fully aware that peaceful sleep is unlikely, but I also know that my dreams will be filled with Damien, every night I dream about everything that happened. It's like watching it on a cinema screen, being on the outside looking in. I will be screaming at the screen saying what will happen and when, but it never changes.

Closing my eyes I start to drift into the memory, it's where I get to be with Damien again. Even though I hate the memory, I love seeing him, touching him, and tasting him. That one kiss was enough for me to know that I want more of him, but for now I only have my dreams and I sleep in torture knowing I will be with him.

Chapter Two

Faith

I HAVE BEEN in this room for 4 weeks now. Whilst it's only been 1 week since Damien said he would get us out of here, I so want to believe him but I haven't seen him. Only the other guy, he's the one who is bringing me my meals, and taking me to the bathroom. As the days go by I am losing all hope of ever getting out of here.

Today started out like the rest, the door to the room being opened and the guy bringing in my breakfast. Porridge and a bottle of orange juice, I can't stand porridge but when you know it's all you get, you eat it.

The door closes with a bang, I wonder what's pissed him off.

I hate being here I just want to go home. It's not that it's terrible, I have not been chained, beaten or raped. The only thing they have done is raise their voice and that was only in the beginning when I was reluctant to do as they asked; but since then nothing. Even so, I can't take this much longer.

I am taken to the bathroom after my breakfast, the shower is running when we get there.

As always, everything is already set up for me, I can switch a shower on myself but no, apparently I'm not trusted to do even that.

"You have 15 minutes!" he yells at me angrily, I wonder what's stuck up his arse. As he closes the bathroom door, I stick my tongue out at his back, my little act of rebellion is pathetic, but it's mine. After using the toilet I step into the shower. It's by no means luxurious; it's lukewarm at best and it's just more than a trickle, but I make do finding the shower gel. I quickly wash my hair and body, what wouldn't I give for some conditioner, is it so much to ask when you kidnap someone make sure you have conditioner? My hair is a bloody mess. I finish up and step from the shower and dry myself putting on the clean t-shirt and jogging bottoms.

Thankfully I am dressed when the door slams open, "Come on, time's up!" He says. His tone is harder than before, I feel his grip on my arm, it's not normally this hard. I don't say anything as he pulls me back towards the bedroom. Pushing me into the room, I land on my hands and knees on the floor, I start to get a feeling of dread settle in my stomach. As I start pulling myself up, he smirks at me as he closes and locks the door as he leaves.

I am still sat on the bed with my knees pulled up to my chest, my arms wrapped around my legs, my head buried in my knees, when the door opens, I look up and see him carrying a tray, dinner time? After what happened earlier I don't feel like eating. Expecting him to leave the door open, to just pop the tray on the bed. I find it odd that he has closed the door.

Making his way over to the bed, he dumps the plastic tray on the bed, it's the same bottle of water and sandwich on the plate, burying my head in my knees again, I expect him to turn around and leave.

My body jumps when I feel his hand on my head, his grip tightens, pulling my hair to make me look at him, "It's playtime princess. It's just you and me now." It takes me a second to process what he is saying. My arms automatically come to my head to try and break his hold but it's no use. He has hold of me and pulls me down by my hair "Please don't, you don't have to do this! I haven't done anything," My arms are moving frantically as he keeps pulling me by my hair, I hear the tray crash to the floor but I don't care, he's pulling me so that I am lying down on the bed, his body trying to cover mine. "Stop, please!" I beg him it's no use he is not listening, his other arm comes up to grab hold of my throat squeezing tightly "Don't stop fighting Faith, it's only making me harder." Oh God I feel sick, the arm that had hold of my hair lets go and he brings his mouth to mine, I refuse to open my mouth.

His body manages to cover mine and his weight is suffocating. I don't know if it's the hand around my throat or the weight of him that makes me see spots. I use the last bit of my strength to spit in his face, I feel his fist connect with my nose "You little bitch" he screams.

I start to struggle again but he is quicker and stronger. He lets go of me and I start to kick and hit him as he tries to get my pants down. I fight so hard to try and keep them on.

It's no use he manages to tug them down, he moves to sit on my stomach trapping my arms against my sides. I can't move, I try to buck and kick but he is immovable. He starts to unbuckle his jeans as I feel the tears fill my eyes. Grabbing hold of himself he starts to stroke his cock "I am going to enjoy this" he chuckles to himself as he continues to get himself off. He grabs my t-shirt forcefully ripping then squeezes my breast hard, the tears are streaming down my face at this point I feel so helpless, I'm trapped.

The door bursts open slamming against the wall "Get your fucking hands off her Conner!"

It's Damien. Thank God. Once the weight has gone from my stomach, I scramble myself into a ball as quick as I can, looking across the room I see Damien has Conner held against the wall.

"What the fuck is your problem" Conner rasps as Damien's hand tightens around his throat.

"You don't get to touch her" I hear his strained reply

I hear a sickening crunch and Conner slides to the floor. Damien turns around and makes his way over to the bed; he looks distressed, it's then I look down and notice that my t-shirt is ripped and my pants are still down. I grab hold of the pants and tug them up as best I can, with being sat on a bed. Clutching the remains of the t-shirt tight to cover my chest I sit there with the tears still flowing, thankful that it is over.

"Faith come on. I am going to get you out of here now" he says.

"Ok" I whisper as he scoops me up off the bed, carrying me down the narrow hall he starts to climb a set of stairs, at the top of the stairs I notice that we are in a kitchen walking out of the back door. He places me in a black SUV, fastening my seatbelt for me he places a kiss on my head "Sorry" he whispers, if I had not been paying attention I would have missed it.

Looking up at what has been my prison for the past month, I notice it's nothing more than a Victorian end terrace house. Figures.

We are driving along the streets I notice that we are driving towards London city center, wondering where he is taking me I decide to ask, pretty sure I can find my voice now.

"Where are we going?" I ask looking over to his side of the SUV.

"Hospital" his one word reply irks me.

"Where have you been all week?" I really want him to talk to me, tell me anything.

"Busy, look Faith I am sorry about what happened back there but you're safe now" his tone told me not to push further.

Parking in the hospital he comes around to my side, opening the door I step down so that I am stood looking up at him.

"Thank you for saving me and getting me out" I step up on my toes and place a chaste kiss on his lips.

"Oh fuck" he whispers against my lips, his hands come to the side of my face being oh so gentle, he captures my lips and I don't hesitate for a second when his tongue traces my lips seeking entry, I respond to his kiss but as soon as it starts it stops.

Walking towards the door to A&E, I get the strange feeling again, and when I look at him I know he is not coming in with me.

"Don't go home" then he turns and leaves me at the doors.

I don't even think about what he said as I make my way into that hospital. I almost collapsed when I reached the reception, a couple of nurses came and took me straight to a room and got me out of my torn clothes and into a hospital gown "Are you ok, what happened?" they asked me.

I stay quiet, not knowing what to tell them. Do I tell them, the truth? Who would even believe me? Surely that would only get Damien in trouble, and I don't want that. He saved me.

"The doctor will be in shortly" the other nurse said once I was settled on the bed. The doctor came and checked me over from head to toe. I only spoke to say my name and ask them to contact Camilla Ashford, no one else but Cami.

He tells me that I have a broken nose and a few scrapes but apart from that I'm fine but they want to keep me in overnight purely because they think I'm in shock.

Cami arrives with a flurry as, she rushes into the room and wraps her arms around me.

"What happened, sweetie are you ok?" I break down and tell her everything that had happened over the last month while she sits at the side of my hospital bed and listens.

"Well I will tell you this for sure, you will be coming home with me and I won't take no for an answer."

"Thanks Camilla, it means a lot." She kisses the top of my head as she gets up to leave.

"I will be back to pick you up in the morning and Faith, stop calling me Camilla you know I hate it. It's Cami."

Giggling as she leaves I know she hates Camilla, for as long as we have been at school together, she would often call me out on it.

The next morning I wake to find Cami already sat by my bed, my nose feels huge this morning, I can still feel the crusty blood around it I must look a right mess.

"Ready to go? The doctor said you could go home."

"Thanks Cami, I am so lucky to have a good friend like you."

Leaving the hospital we the drive from the hospital to Chelsea where her apartment is. She lets me in and shows me to the guest room and I am in awe. The king size bed with cream and duck egg bedding and cream and silver bird wallpaper fills the room, a chic dresser and stool are on the opposite wall to the bed. I spy a door in the corner.

I walk through the door to a beautiful ensuite bathroom which is filled with a beautiful lion claw tub and corner shower. I look at her and she just nods letting me know it's real.

It's then I wake from my tortured dream. The same dream I have every night.

In the light of day I know what I need to do to sort this mess out the one person who can help me and keep me safe.

I need to find Damien.

CHAPTER THREE

Damien

THE DRIVE TO the penthouse is hell, I always stop by Faith's building, anything to be closer to her. It never makes the ache go away though, if anything, it only makes it worse. I arrive at home closing the door to my apartment, blocking out the world so I can have my thoughts consumed by Faith. The ringing phone pulls my attention from my tortured thoughts.

"What?" I bark as I answer the phone.

"Sir, just letting you know we have traced Darren Young" I could hear the relief in his voice, I had driven them hard this past 6 months trying to find him.

"Well it's about fucking time, where is he?" I ask Malcolm.

"He was flagged at Gatwick airport this morning, he's back in London sir. What do you want us to do?" he asks, he already knows what I want.

"Find out where he goes, we need to form a plan first." I heard his moan of protest, then the line cut off. I could not wait to kill the lowlife scumbag. I despised the man, what kind of man would give his daughter away to settle a debt.

I know Malcolm will do as I asked, they all do without a second thought.

My men are trained, and they're loyal. Most importantly, they understand the chain of command.

I never wanted this job in the beginning, I mean who really wants to be the head of their family? To be in control of an empire. I certainly didn't. When you grow up surrounded by the family's dealings, watching your own father kill people there is a certain expectation, and there is fuck all you can do about it. So I do what I was born and raised to do. I lead and people follow. Otherwise it would be me six feet under now, not my father.

I have been keeping an eye on Faith and she hardly leaves the apartment, except on a Thursday to go see her therapist and even then her friend takes her straight there and straight back, she is a shell of who she was before..

I ached to go to her, to comfort her, but I know I can't. So I watch over her, I don't want her to see me I just want her to forget and move on. I want her to be happy.

It kills me staying away from her, but I know it's wrong to want her. I can't help it, after I had her captured I thought it would be ok, that I would be able to go through with it.

It started off fine, she was in that room and everything was going smoothly, at least while she was out cold that is.

The moment she woke and I saw her huddled in the corner, I was doomed. She looked so helpless. It was then that the vision of my sister locked in that room tied and beaten to a pulp, lying in her own blood that I decided Faith would not meet the same fate. I would make sure of it.

I head towards the shower needing to get ready for tonight. We have a little surprise visit arranged with another hotshot who thinks it's ok to take my money and not pay it back. Resting my head against the shower wall, I close my eyes and take a breath, I can't help but see her face in that kitchen window. She looked broken, and I had done that to her.

It was mum's old house that I had taken her to, it had been empty for the last six years since Bella had died.

It was looking run down and unkempt, but the Victorian house had a cellar that was just what I needed, dark and dirty.

I had tried not to let her in but it was impossible.

I even tried to stay away for that last week. That proved to be useless as Conner thought with me not around he could get his dick wet. I saw red when I walked into that room and Conner on top of her, the look of fear I saw on her face as the tears slid down her cheek, I didn't hesitate to get him the fuck off her.

Well let's just say he won't be using it anymore, I made sure of that. I enjoyed every minute of the torture

I put him through as soon as I had dropped her off at the hospital. I drove back to the house where he was still passed out on the floor. The satisfaction I got when he came round tied up and stripped naked. “You know what happens to rapists?” That was the only time I spoke to him, his screams to my dying day will not haunt me. They give me a sense of peace, knowing that I avenged Faith even if she doesn’t know it. No one hurts my Faith.

I strip down in my bathroom, the room is huge the shower easily big enough to fit 4 people inside but I only think about having one person in here with me.

When I step into the shower the water is pounding down hard against my back, my head leaning against the wall, as always thoughts of my girl still invading my every thought.

Looking down I’m as hard as granite, I know I shouldn’t but I can’t help it I reach down and close my hand round my erection, I start to move my hand up and down. The thoughts of Faith spread out on my bed cause me to work myself faster and harder, I keep going and with that last vision I have of myself sinking deep inside her, I fall over the edge. My climax hitting the shower wall before my body sags as I come back down.

Arriving later at the warehouse, I can still hear the muffled cries from the back of the van we are in. I look at Malcolm; he knows what we are here to do. It’s become all too familiar over the past six years it’s part of the job and I won’t let muscle do a job that I can do myself.

I do have some morals, I am not a total monster. I only hurt people when they have done wrong or won't pay up then I may use little incentives to help them make the right decision; like with Darren we had given warning after warning and he had said that he would come up with the money. Taking Faith was a last resort she was just supposed to be there a day or two making her dad want to pay up to get her back. But then the fucker turned the tables and told us to take her as payment. It was with that phone call and the decision was made, his life would come to an end.

I let my thoughts come back to the here and now and I get on with pulling this arsehole from the back of the van. Someone else that thinks he can borrow money and not pay it back. It should be pretty easy to deal with this prick.

Inside the bland room, it's empty of any furniture but a chair and the yellow tarp that the chair sits on.

Malcolm ties him to the chair so that he can't get up and run away. How am I supposed to teach him a lesson if he runs away? Pulling the tape from his mouth he lets out a deep breath. He knows why he is here, after repeated warnings he's still not paid what he owes. That's not something that I can just let slide. It can't go unpunished.

"Look don't do this, I have the money I will pay please don't do this" as he finishes speaking I give Malcolm a bored look as I bring the butt of my gun had across his face. "You know you're not leaving here without learning a little lesson," I speak directly to him looking him in the eyes so I can see when his eyes widen in fear and realisation.

His pleas fall on deaf ears, to be honest I am sick of hearing it. I have better things to be doing than teaching some scumbag not to piss me off by avoiding payment. When will people learn? You borrow, you pay back, simple really he needs to be taught a lesson, and that's exactly what I intend to do.

I hear the echo of a gunshot and see his body go limp on the chair. Malcolm always enjoys ending it. After we had taken our time beating him, listening to him beg a moment longer was going to drive me insane. That's when I gave Malcolm the nod.

"Get rid of him, and make sure he is not easy to find."

There would be nothing in the way of evidence to tie this to me, but all those who know me, would know it was a message.

Heading out of the warehouse I go to my car that we left here earlier, oh I love this car, it's not just a car. It's a Bentley Continental Gt in gunmetal grey, with full leather seats inside. My pride and joy love driving her to the house in Surrey, I hate the penthouse in London and only stay for work, being closer to the city for business is always better in case anything goes wrong.

I was just getting into the car when I heard Malcolm begin speaking behind me.

"Boss, we have a problem with Faith, she has had the old bill at hers tonight, Jake just called me to let me know." At his words I spin around. *What the fuck have I missed?*

"What, the fuck is going on Malc? Start talking. Now."

"Boss, Jake said no one but old bill been there so no present danger to her. What do you want us to do?"

"Nothing yet, you clear this up first. Then we discuss Faith when you are back at the penthouse, do I make myself clear."

He nods and steps away as I turn and get into the car. I knew leaving the new man watching her had been a mistake, I won't forgive myself if anything has happened to her. I start the car and set off towards the house.

Arriving back at the penthouse I pace in the living room. The urge to go and get her is driving me insane because I can't help the feeling that something is wrong. There is this feeling in the pit of my stomach and it just won't go away, it's clawing at me from the inside.

When Malc gets back he wanders over to the living room where I am sat in the chair, three shots of whiskey seemed to help calm me down a little bit.

"What do you want to do D? We have her being watched, we have Darren being watched what else can we do?" he sounds pissed off and I'm not really surprised. I've been obsessed with her safety for the last six months since I dropped her off. I know that she thinks I left her but I never did, I couldn't. Malcolm knows what happened with my sister and my dad, he has been with me since we were young, we even went to primary school together so he understands why I am so desperate to keep her safe.

"I will tell you what I want shall I? I want her with me." I told him his face was a mixture of shock and outrage.

"Oh you're really funny! You can't be serious? We've discussed this, that's why we keep her safe from a distance. Do you honestly think she will be ok with everything that's going on?" his question through me for a second but I've made up my mind.

"I don't care Malc I want her here with me where she belongs."

"Do you think she will ever be ok with knowing that it was you who kidnapped her? You can't keep it from her if she's here!"

"I don't care Malc I need to keep her safe at least until the threat has gone"

"She could hate you Damien" his last comment did stun me for a minute but I quickly shook it off. I don't care what he thinks. He's paid to do as I tell him, not to question me.

My last thought before I leave the living room bidding him a goodnight is that I am going to get my girl!

Chapter Four

Faith

I'M SITTING AT the kitchen island eating my grapefruit and having my coffee when Cami strolls in she grabbed herself a cup of coffee from the pot and sits down beside me.

"How are you feeling this morning?" she sounds nervous like she's scared of my answer.

"Believe it or not Cami, I'm ok." she looks at me like I've grown a third eye or something, is it really that hard to believe?

I've been seeing that therapist and had only spoken to Cam about everything that happened to me so yes I can understand why she looks so shocked.

"Ok, so we're going out for lunch today then?" she asks.

She's sneaky I will give her that, she was testing me and I knew it.

"Great! Where are we going?" I said with a false sense of confidence. I plastered a fake smile on my face. She knew what I was doing when the amused smile lit up her face.

"Think we will just go to the little café up the road what do you say"

"Fantastic" I said sarcastically I get up and male my way back to my bedroom what the bloody hell am I doing thinking of going out after last night.

I was determined this morning to not let it get to me. I have spent the last six months hiding from the world I can't keep doing it. Nothing else has happened since, the fear is all in my head.

I switch on the shower wanting to get ready for the day ahead. I am not going to let fear rule me any longer. I am done, it is time to take my life back.

Stepping inside the shower I wash quickly before I can let my mind wander back to last night, if it did, I'd start to panic and get anxious again.

I wrap the towel around my body and wander back to my bedroom. The mirrored wardrobe is open on the one side so that I can see some of my dresses and jeans that are hung there.

I notice my skinny jeans, walking over I pulled them from the hanger and start sifting through for a top to wear. I decide on a light pink sheath top with butterflies on it.

I blow out my blonde hair and leave it loose, applying only a little bit of make-up. I hate the girls who pile it on thick, it just looks horrible. When you see the orange lines around their chins and up to their hairlines. For God sake can they not see when they apply it that it's three shades too dark? Bit of mascara eyeliner and lip balm and I am good to go.

Back in the living room I find Cami ready and waiting to go. She really is pretty. Her sleek black bob with the light blue tips that match her eyes, she was a good few inches smaller than my 5ft 7in frame.

Her black leggings and grey off the shoulder jumper she wore made her slight curves seem fuller. It really was a good look on her she had topped it off with her trademark heels. She loved her heels; Cami had them in all colours and designs. Luckily for her we weren't the same size feet anymore or I would still be stealing them like I used to back in university.

Whenever there was a party and we would need to get dressed up, she never failed to lend me some of her amazing shoes. I had worn every possible designer, it just showed how selfless she was, even back then she would always share or offer anyone help.

"Wow look at you Faith! You look like your old self" she says to me with nothing but honesty in her voice.

"Thanks, Cami you look amazing"

"Don't thank me just yet we are making a little detour before lunch." she looked me straight in the eyes daring me to say something back or wimp out but instead I just nod and walk to the closet to grab my jacket, leaving a speechless Cami behind me.

Inside I was shaking, the fear trying to creep back in, I blew out a breath while waiting at the front door for Cami.

Walking towards the café, I couldn't help but look at everyone. I was sure everybody was staring at me, Cami looped my arm and pulled me a little closer to her while we continued walking down the street.

Stopping abruptly she said, "we're here" I looked up and noticed that we were at a nice little hairdressers. Pulling me inside she walked right up to the reception desk. Before I had time to act, Cami had booked me in; I was taken to a chair where a gown was put around my shoulders. The next thing the stylist comes over "what can we do for you today sweetie."

I just stare at her in the mirror in front of me "um can I just have a trim and my layers cut back in please" I ask quietly

"Of course sweetie" her reply puts me at ease a little and I relax into the chair while she makes quick work of my hair.

Forty minutes later. Cami and I leave the salon. I must say it's been a while since my hair has looked this good, it feels heavenly I keep running my fingers through it, I can't help it as it's so soft and silky.

Walking through the door, we find a little table along the sidewall of the cafe it's a little place. White chairs and tables are dotted around the space with red and white table covers on them. Little vases filled with artificial flowers inside of them. The whole little café gives off that cosy feel. Taking a seat I start to look at the menu. It's been that long since I have been in here that I have forgotten what is on it.

I notice the waitress as she comes over, so I wait for Cami to make her order so I can just order the same.

"What can I get you girls?" she asks

“I will have a lasagne with salad please and a lemonade” Cami tells the waitress. She then looks over to me waiting for my order so I just say that I will have the same. After writing the order down, she heads back over to her station to sort our drinks.

The wait for our food was not that long and we make small talk while waiting. When our lasagne was put down in front of us, I cannot believe how hungry I was and could not wait to tuck in, it smelled amazing.

The cheese was grilled perfectly on top, the side salad looked very crisp and fresh.

Picking up my fork I tuck in to my dinner, I know what’s coming, so I brace myself ready to answer her questions.

“So what’s the real reason for the change in you today Faith?” Cami questioned me.

“What do you mean, I’m just trying to get on with my life Cami, to take control again”

“Ha. Don’t make me bloody laugh. You have only left the apartment to go and see your therapist. Every time I bring up the question of going outside you close up like a clam, so don’t you dare say to me that you just got up this morning and thought fuck it! I’m fine!”

“You know I only let you get away with speaking to me like that because I love you, I know what you must think and there is a reason why which I will tell you if you let me get a word in.”

“Well don’t let me stop you,” Cami said to me

“I need to find Damien.” I just said it was no point beating around the bush.

“Are you out of your fucking mind? Why on earth would you want to find him?” her voice had raised an octave as she was talking and people in the café were starting to look at us.

"Keep your voice down please." I plead with her, was it not enough that I was saying this outside of the apartment?

"Look I know you don't understand why, but he saved me Cami, you know the details I'm not rehashing it here" I dropped my voice to a whisper so that only Cami could hear "I love him."

I heard the clatter of her fork as it hits the table. The utter shock was written across her face.

"Don't be stupid Faith, you don't know him so how can you love him! Why won't you get that he kept you there, he helped whoever took you he is as bad as the rest of them."

I refuse to listen to what she was saying I know what happened. I live it every night but I also know that he was kind to me, that he seemed to care for me. I got to shower, eat and drink, I had a feeling that if it was not for him I would not have had those things.

"Look just stop. Cami, I am going to find him with or without your help, I know you don't understand and I doubt you ever will, but I need you as my best friend to help me, please." I look at her hoping that she can see the truth in my eyes. She is my best friend and I love her so much I have a feeling I won't be able to do this without her.

"Urgh! Fine. I will help you try to find him, but only because I love you and if I don't you will probably do something stupid."

I leave the conversation at that and we finish up eating dinner. Even though I have been out with Cami who is my safety net it is not as hard as I thought it was going to be. Maybe I can be me again one day.

The walk back to the apartment is nice and peaceful, there is a nice breeze but it's not chilly, it's pleasant. The blue sky, fluffy white clouds and the sunshine give off the feel of a summer's day. While walking back we make plans to do this again on Thursday after my next therapy session.

Walking up the stairs to the apartment, giggling I can't remember that last time we had a carefree afternoon, opening the door our fun comes crashing to an end when we walk into the living room.

"Hello Princess," I shudder at the nickname as I see the man I once called dad sat watching us come through the door.

"What are you doing here?" I glare at him how dare he show up here after what he did to me.

"We are going home Faith, and you are coming with me." I recoil away from him.

"I am not going anywhere with you! You told them to keep me for your debt. How could you do that me?" I start to raise my voice, how dare he even be here. I don't want him anywhere near me.

"You are and you will Faith! Your little escape still means I have a debt to settle, you think he will forget that I owe him money."

"Get out" I scream at him "I don't want you anywhere near me do you understand! I don't care who you owe money to I am not a part of that."

I notice Cami is stood frozen like a deer in headlights not knowing what to do for the best. He stands and starts to make his way towards me, totally ignoring Cami and I am grateful for that at least, I would never forgive myself if anything happened to Cami because of me.

I start to back up towards the front door while he still strides towards me, he looks possessed, not the man that I knew as my father.

"You owe me everything you spoiled little bitch, I paid for everything you ever had school, clothes, cars, and university, you will do and go where I say you will."

His grip on my arm halts my backwards steps, the resounding slap across my face causes me to bite down on my lip, the blood that now trickles down my chin when I bring myself to look at him again. His eyes widen with fear, he drops my arm like it has burned him and takes a step back. The hairs on my neck stand on end, as I become aware of the presence behind me. I whip myself around to see who has put that fear into my father, I lock onto deep caramel eyes and gasp.

"Hello Faith." *Oh God that voice.*

Damien.

Chapter Five

Faith

"DAMIEN?" I BREATHE, my chest constricts at the sight of him finding that I have lost my voice. The flood of memories that assault my mind, all my dreams and that kiss collide.

I don't hear the commotion that's going on around me until I feel his arms wrap around me pulling me closer and pushing me behind so he is in front protecting me, from what is happening around us.

I hear the high pitch scream from Cami and when I look up I see that my dad is using her as a shield with a knife at her throat.

"Dad what are you doing" I screech at him while trying to get around Damien but his hold on me is like an iron grip.

"Let her go please" I plead with him, hoping to see some humanity in his eyes but I only see hate.

"Oh no, I don't think I will be letting her go she is my ticket out of here alive, I need to even up the odds" his words are filled with such venom.

Looking around my apartment I notice that there are another two men with Damien they flank him on both sides.

"Darren you don't want to do anything stupid. Let the girl go." Damien's voice still sends a flash of arousal straight to my core, his tone is commanding but sensual at the same time, I can't help but imagine him whispering sweet nothings to me.

"Oh I think I know what I am doing" every word out of his mouth is making me itch to go and punch him, and I'm not a violent person but the action and words of my so called father are making me see red.

I hate that he is using my best friend to help him get out of here. Cami's heaving chest and tears are eating me up inside and all I want to do is go to her and take her place it should be me he uses not her she has not done anything wrong.

His grip tightens on Cami and she lets out a strangled whimper, I flinch when I hear her.

"You're not walking out of here Darren" I hear his words and I gasp, shocked at the malice in his words.

"See that's where you're wrong you have Faith back Damien, so the debt is settled now, I am going to take Cami with me and if anyone tries to stop me I will kill her" he finishes speaking.

That's when I realise what he actually said, no it's not right it can't be, Damien got me out, oh God I feel sick Damien says something to one of the men and he starts to advance on my Dad and Cami.

"STOP. Don't come any closer, or I will slit her pretty little throat"

Damien's man does not stop he carries on getting closer and I see my dad press the dagger firmly into Cami's neck. I see the slight trickle of blood glide down her throat as the point of the blade pierces the skin

"DAMIEN!" I scream

"Tell your man to stop! He is hurting Cami please Damien get him to stop" I start to sob now as I see the blood on Cami she is my rock, I can't lose her it seems like an age until Damien's man stops his fists clenched at his sides, like he is finding it extremely hard to hold himself back.

"Faith you tell Damien to let me past, if not I will kill Cami, you know I will do it." He knows how much I love Cami. She is and always will be my best friend, these past 6 months have made us even closer and I would trade places in an instant with her.

"Let him go, please Damien, I can't lose Cami, please just let him leave I will do whatever you want, just let him go."

I look at him pleading with him to understand that I need this from him I need him to let my father walk out of here so I can keep Cami alive.

"Malcolm, Jake, let him past." he commands. He looks outraged that he has to let him go. I am relieved that he listened to me.

I see my dad start to move Cami toward the front door of the apartment, I see Damien's men, whose names I now know as Malc and Jake, one is young about 24 my age he has light brown hair and blue eyes he is nowhere near as built as Damien or the other guy. I mean they look like they should be models not here doing whatever the hell it is they do. The other guy is huge and I mean army shaved head he just looks mean he won't take his eyes off Cami, like all he wants to do is get her away, he has that look that screams protector.

They let my dad pass with Cami still in front of him and the blade still digging into her neck.

"At least you can still do as your told Faith, nobody try anything." I hear Cami's crying and heaving breaths as she leaves the apartment, he is shouting at her to walk down the stairs.

I bury my face into Damien's chest and start to cry; I can't believe I let her leave with him oh my God what have I done. I feel his arms holding me closer to him.

"Malc. Find her" Damien commands I turn my head to the side, just in time to see the huge guy with the shaved head fly out of my apartment door and down the stairs.

Damien leads me back into the living room of the apartment and sits me down on the couch, I am shaking with fear for Cami, I notice that he is tense and stiff, I am watching him trying to control himself, I think he feels helpless and angry, I am just about to put my hand on his lap to try and soothe him when he stands abruptly.

He starts walking over to the other man Jake, I only know this because a few seconds ago he sent Malc out to find my girl.

"You should have been watching her better! I told you nothing and I mean nothing was to happen to her" he has Jake pinned against the wall the anger is rolling off him. His fist punches him right in the face and he starts to go to work on him.

"I'm sorry Boss it won't happen again" his speech it's mumbled probably by the swelling in his face or it's hoarse from the air being squeezed out of his body, just then I realise what he said and my dad's words fill my head again. You have her back debt paid and then Jake just now calling Damien boss. What the fuck! Before I know what I am doing I'm up off the couch hitting Damien's back repeatedly "This is all your fault" I keep screaming this at him.

Dropping the poor guy on the floor he spins around picking me up, all the anger leaves his face as soon as he sees it's me and he places me back on the couch. He sits beside me, I shuffle away from him. I want answers.

After a few moments I try to calm myself enough to get my questions out.

"What did he mean when he said you had me back so the debt is settled?" I can see the guilt that is written across his face.

"Look it's not what you think I will tell you but not now we have to get you somewhere safe."

I am about to answer when I hear crying coming from the hall I turn to see Malc carrying Cami in his arms he strides into the living room, she looks even smaller in his arms, he places her down on the couch, I rush over to her and I am so relieved that she is ok and here, not lying in a ditch somewhere dead.

"Oh God, Cami, I'm so sorry, I'm so sorry" I crouch down by the side of the couch holding her hand while I speak, stroking her hair with my free hand.

"Are you ok let me see your neck Cami please did he do anything else."

She shakes her head and tilts it so I can see the wound on her neck. The cut is not a huge gaping hole like I was imagining but it is still a mark on her skin that should never have been put there, a tap on my shoulder alerts me to the first aid kit that Malc passes me, I open the first aid kit and get to work cleaning up my best friends wound.

The only thing that I know for certain at this moment in time is that Damien is not who I thought Cami is hurt but safe for now, my father is dead to me but I have a feeling this is far from over. Looking at my best friend I see the fear in her eyes and I know that I have caused it.

"Faith" my name is but a whisper upon her lips, I squeeze her hand so she knows she has my attention.

"Darren said this was not over and that he won't be happy till you're back with him or dead" I gasp at her words.

"Ssshhhh it's ok Cami you safe now" I don't know where I get the strength to say it but I know she needs reassurance and that's what I give her.

We sit there in silence until Cami has drifted off to sleep. I notice that Malc has not left her side, I think he feels more guilt than I do. I need to talk to Damien. I need to know what the hell is going on. I get up placing her hand on the couch, kissing her on the forehead as I turn to leave to go and face Damien.

"You can't stay here Faith I will not allow it." How fucking dare he try and command this situation after everything he has done.

"That is not your choice to make, and you still owe me an explanation for all this shit that's going on Damien. How the hell did you know where I live? Why are you here?"

"I'm not doing this here, we have to leave now." he orders again and it is pissing me off

"Tell me." I demand.

"Fine, you want to know? I will tell you. I took you. Are you happy? Your dad owed me a lot of money, I wanted to scare him into paying up, but when the fucker said to keep you, I couldn't do it." His words rock me back into that hell and I hate him for causing this but I have to know why, I'm not scared of him.

"Why?" it's the only thing I say. He knows what I'm asking.

"I can't answer that here. Now I have answered your question, go and pack a bag or I will pack it for you. We are leaving here now, you said you would do anything if I let him walk out. I did that, so this is what I want, you with me."

You have got to be kidding me, he can't just expect me to up and leave with him. He fucking kidnapped me! He can't be serious, but one look at him and I know that he is. Thinking back over what has happened this afternoon, how can I stop that happening myself? I can't. I won't be able to do anything about it. Until all of this blows over, I need to be with Damien.

"Cami comes as well or I don't leave, do you understand. And before you get any funny ideas don't you dare take me back to that hellhole of a house,"

He does not even acknowledge me with words just a nod of his head, he picks up his phone and makes some calls I'm not sure what about and to be honest I don't care. My head is all over the place and I realise that I am not even close to being over this.

"You may want to pack yourself and Cami a bag" it's Malc that speaks to me and I'm a little shocked at his accent I can't place, it seems Russian or somewhere similar, it's soothing believe it or not.

Cami is still asleep on the couch and I wonder if she will be ok. I head to her room and pack her a bag, some toiletries and clothes to see her over for a few days I turn to see Malc behind me I pass him her bag and head to my own room to pack.

Looking in my drawers and wardrobe I take out some jeans and t-shirts grabbing my make-up throwing it all into the bag opening my underwear drawer, I grab a couple of bras and knickers not caring what they look like.

Heading back into the living room the tension is high, you could cut the atmosphere with a knife. I place my bag down next to Cami and he knows I'm ready to go.

"Malc is going to take Cami and Jake to the house, you are going to ride with me so we can talk, ok?"

I don't miss the smile that hints on his lips and I won't say that his words don't cause heat to spread to my core, because they do, I won't deny that after all I have heard today, I know I should not want him but my body betrays me, it sets on fire when he's near me.

"Fine" I say happy at the chance to finally get the answers that I want, that I feel I need in order to put all this shit behind me, and try to get a sense of my normal life back.

"I will keep you safe Faith I will find your Father and when I do I will kill him he won't walk away again and he will never hurt you again" I feel a tug at my heart strings at his words, when he is with me I feel safe and protected.

Jake carries the bags to the cars, Malc walks out of our apartment carrying Cami she started to stir but Malc's soothing words soothed her back to sleep.

We set off heading to wherever the hell it is that we're going. That's something else he has failed to mention to me.

“Damien where are we going?” I ask as we get into his car it’s a really nice looking car, so sleek and sexy.

“My home” is his reply and we are back to being vague.

“And where is that exactly?”

“Surrey, it’s the family home, it’s safe.”

Chapter Six

Damien

I START THE car and head for home, just that one word makes me sigh in relief. I have not been home for 7 months, choosing to use the penthouse so that I could be closer to Faith.

This day has been surreal to say the least, looking across to the passenger seat of the car, checking to make sure she really is sitting there.

She is the light to my dark, good to my evil, and I won't ever let her go.

"Are you ok Faith?" I tentatively ask her.

"What do you think Damien? Really? Come on you're not that dense, I will break it down for you shall I." Oh, I do love it when she gets a bee in her bonnet like this. The fire that lights up in her eyes sends a jolt straight to my cock.

"Please, break it down for me, I would love to hear what you think you know." I think winding her up is going to become my favourite game. She does not even know who I am, yet she stands up to me already.

"Fine, you kidnapped me to settle my father's debt, then you let me go, I spend the next six months looking over my shoulder, then my dad tries to take me, you show up out of the blue. Cami my best friend gets hurt, he gets away and basically you give me no choice but to come with you so yeah I think I got the gist of it, don't you think." her little speech is not that far off the mark but there a few things missing. I'm going to set her straight right now.

"You're wrong Faith, I did not kidnap you to settle his debt, we took you to make him pay up." She just looks at me with utter disdain.

"You think kidnap of any sort, is right do you?" she questions me.

"I have never claimed to be a saint, but I will tell you this. I'm the one that let you go, because what your father did was wrong. Like I'm the one now who is protecting you from him again."

I can feel my temper starting to rise, as we speak about her dickhead of a father. It really does eat away at me that a father could ever do this to his daughter. If I ever have a daughter she will be cherished and guarded. Not to be made a pawn in some game for my advantage.

"Did I ask you to? No, I have not asked for any of this, Damien. I have spent the last six months in therapy and I relive what happened every night. I wake in the night drenched in sweat, because Conner's hands are all over me. And that bloody kiss, then you just left me there, you did not even spare me a glance back."

Her confession rocks me to my very soul, between me and her dad we have broken her.

"I never left you" I whisper my throat constricting with the emotion I am feeling at the minute. If my men saw me now talking about my feelings, they would think I'm a pussy and need to be taken out. In my life you have to be top dog or someone else will be. It's that simple everybody is replaceable.

"It was you, wasn't it, all this time? I thought I was seeing things, I thought I was going crazy."

"You think I wanted to stay in the shadows? No, I did it so you could be safe and move on." The miles are eaten up as we argue in the car; it won't be long until we arrive in Surrey.

"That's bullshit! You know what Damien, just drop it, I don't want to talk about it anymore." I can see the hurt in her eyes the silent tears that roll down her cheeks, so I decide that for now I will drop it, I don't want to hurt her anymore.

"Fine." I grunt, and carry on driving down the motorway, it's not that long of a drive, only about an hour to Godalming in Surrey. The silence in the car for the rest of the trip, is not a peaceful one, I will be glad when I get home.

Slowly crawling up the drive, I pull the car to a stop in front of the house. Stepping out I look up to see the grandeur that is my home, well estate to give you some semblance of the size.

I watch Faith close the door and gape.

"Wow, nice place," she exclaims.

I chuckle at her response, I realise that to some this place is huge and it probably is, but to me it's home, it's the place where I grew up. "Come on let's get you and Cami settled," I nod over to the other car that's parked, letting her know that they have already arrived.

Walking through the door into the entrance hall I see that nothing has changed. The few staff that I have keep the place spotless.

The dark marble floor shines, the cream walls gleam and the table in the middle of the hall is spotless, with the fresh flowers sat on top.

It just shows what money can do; I only rang them just over an hour ago to say that we would be arriving shortly.

"Malc take Cami straight up to one of the guest rooms please, and have the staff fetch her something to eat and drink, once you have her settled we have business that needs discussing." I make my words polite but he knew they were an order.

Looking across to Faith, I need to show her to her room, but the thought of taking her to any other bedroom but mine, does not sit well with me. I have this need to have her in my home and my bed. Well I have her in my home now, now I just need to work on getting her into my bed, cause once I have her there she won't ever be leaving. She is mine.

"Come on Faith I'll take you to where you'll be staying." I don't lead her up the stairs, instead I walk past the living room and the office to the door at the bottom of the hall.

I open the door to the master suite; I walk in and see that nothing has changed the huge four poster king-size bed with the sheath drapes attached to each post. The red and creams in this room give it a warm feel, the dark wood of the dressing table and the side tables are the only masculine parts of the room, the attached dressing room is filled with my suits and jeans and tops I wonder how she is going to react when she sees them.

She wanders round running her hand across the bedding on the bed, God help me, the sight of her there at my bed. My cock is now rock hard straining against my zip to be free. Placing her bag at the foot of the bed she looks in awe at the room I never thought seeing approval in someone else would mean anything to me, but I want to please Faith, I want her to be happy here with me.

"Wow Damien this room is beautiful, it feels cosy and safe." It sends a thrill through me when she says she feels safe in my home.

"Glad you like my bedroom." I want to see her reaction, that's why I say it to her.

"Why am I in your bedroom? I thought you were taking me to the bedroom I would be staying in."

"You are in the room you are staying in." I see her eyes widen at my words. She is wondering the meaning of them. The blush that starts to climb up her neck is sexy as hell. I want to keep putting that blush up her neck. So before she can start to scream and shout I finish speaking.

"Don't worry Faith I won't be staying in here with you unless you want me to?" I give her a smirk when I finish.

"Oh" is all she says to me. I can't help it if it makes me harder. I thought it was going down but hearing little words like that come from her sweet lips. Just makes my cock jump back up ready to say hello.

"Right, I am going to leave you now. I have work to do, but when you're ready feel free to come and find me. The bathroom is through that door over there. If you want a shower or anything."

I turn and leave before the thoughts of her naked body in the shower all wet and soapy get the better of me.

I walk into the office and see Malc and Jake already sat at the desk waiting for me, I walk round to my chair and take my seat, I love my glass desk I can see everything that is under it. Nobody gets the upper hand on me.

The white walls give this room a clean and sterile feel, I think that's what the interior designer said when she was decorating it, I don't remember much of what she was talking about at the time. I think I had her bent over the desk.

Some might say I have been a bit promiscuous with women. I have not stayed with any one woman long; they just never caused a stirring in anything other than my dick. It was a warm place to find release.

I never had to try hard. The women, they flocked to me. Money and power have that effect on people.

"Right I want to know what the fuck happened today, how it all went tits up" I direct my question at Jake, he has pissed me off and I'm not sure that just pinning him against the wall was enough to satisfy the thirst I have for his blood.

"Boss I said I'm sorry. I called as soon as I realised it was Darren. Next time I won't hesitate to take him on."

"You won't get another chance, so don't disappoint me again, if he had harmed her, you would not be sitting here." he nods his head frantically understanding the meaning behind my words. I will kill him if he fucks up again.

"Right Malc, as for you, run it by me again how you got Cami, with everything that went on I might have a few details wrong." Malc tenses up when I mention Cami's name. He looks pissed off all of a sudden. I will have to find out what that is about later when Jake is not around, and it's just him, whiskey and me.

"I went after her like you said to. I ran down the stairs of the apartment. When I got out of the building he was dragging her towards his car the knife was hanging at his side, so I knew he had no hold of Camilla other than his hand, so I crept up behind him, when he got to his car he had her half pinned to the car, he was fumbling with his keys when I hit him on the back of the head with my gun. He slumped forward and I picked up Camilla and brought her back upstairs the rest you know." His explanation was as I expected. The only thing that pissed me off was the fact that he was still breathing. He won't be for long. I will personally end his life. I will take great pleasure in knowing that I control his final breath.

"That's fine, what we need to do now is find him, you know that he will go underground and hide again, I want him found use every resource we have available to us, I want him in 48 hours."

Both men nod and stand to leave my office, to get on with the task I have set them.

Walking into the kitchen I see Faith sat at the table with a drink in her hand. She is sat looking out of the window that has a view of the garden at the back of the house. She does not turn to me when I get closer to her. I see the silent heave of her chest and my breath catches. The sudden feeling of helplessness that I cannot fix gets a tight grip of me.

"I know why you took me Damien, and I hate my father for what he has caused, and I know you will kill him when you find him, I overheard you in your office when I came downstairs, I listened to how Malc saved Cami and how you told them to find him." I crouch down in front of her and lift her chin with my fingers stroking the pad of my thumb across her bottom lip, and it's then when I look into her eyes wet with the tears that have fallen for a family that she no longer has.

She is not weak or helpless, she is a fighter, and she is in a house with a man who had kidnapped her. A ruthless man with a fucked up moral compass. She knows I am a killer and yet she does not pull away from my touch.

I look in to her eyes she knows what I am about to do. I look for any sign that she doesn't want me to kiss her. She gives me a slight nod as I bring my lips down to hers, gently at first, waiting for her to respond to my touch. I gingerly press my tongue against the seam of her mouth, hoping she grants me entry. I have waited 6 months to feel her lips against mine again. The last kiss was fast and furious this one is slow and tender. I think I am trying to show her that there is more to me than what she has seen. With this kiss I pour all my emotions that I feel for her into it. I explore every little part of her mouth with my tongue. I move my hand to her cheeks so I can get even closer to her. She tastes divine. Better than the brief taste I got before I left her.

I break the kiss and just look into her eyes. I see straight into her soul, it's pure and whole. Not tainted by death, lies or deceit. She will either help save me, or break me. But I don’t care I will take anything she freely gives me.

“I need you Faith,” I whisper against her lips. God help anyone who tries to take her from me.

Chapter Seven

Faith

I PULL AWAY when he breathes those words against my lips, I don't know what to do, and I want him so much. I ache to feel his hands all over my body his lips pressing soft kisses against my skin, his fingers pressing hard into my soft flesh.

Would it be wrong to give in just this once to feel connected to him, I need to forget the pain.

I lift my hand and place them on his cheeks, I see the pain in his eyes. I don't want to see it I want to erase it. So I forget my thoughts and follow what my body wants. I bring my lips inches from his. Wanting him to know that I need this as much as he does.

"You have me." I say to him. The change is instant, he grips me harder pulling me to stand with him, I don't fight I follow where he leads. His lips come down against mine, harder this time. Passion flows through the kiss, he lifts me up and I wrap my legs around his waist, all the while he is kissing me, I grip onto him tighter while he carries me out of the kitchen.

I don't remember much about getting to his bedroom. His lips never leave mine as he gently places me down on the bed.

His hands pull off my pink sheath top exposing my plain white cotton bra, shit I had forgotten I wore this plain set, well come to think about it, when I got ready this morning I didn't think I would be having sex tonight that's for sure.

He pops the button open on my jeans and pulls the zip down slowly, while his mouth is laying tender kisses down my stomach, his hands grip the waist band of my jeans and he gently tugs them down, I lift my arse slightly to make it easier for him.

With my jeans off I am left in my white thong and bra. His breath against my skin causes it to get goose pimples.

"You're stunning Faith. I have dreamt about this so many times," he says against my stomach. It's in this moment, I don't care that this should not be happening.

His kisses burn my skin they make me feel alive. He starts trailing them across my hips, he is getting lower, his fingers go to pull my thong down and I tense up, he stops suddenly looking at me. I suddenly feel very exposed, the memory of what Conner tried to do to me, and the fact that I'm still a virgin is starting to make me feel ashamed of myself. How can a man like Damien, who is so commanding and strong, want someone shy and pathetic like me?

“What’s wrong?” his concern is sweet but how do I tell him? How do I tell him that I had visions of Conner holding me down and the fact that I’m a virgin? I have messed around in college and stuff but never all the way. It never bothered me until right now. I want that intimacy with Damien.

I turn my head so I can look into his eyes as I speak to him.

“I’m ok Damien. I just don’t know what happens now. I have never really done anything like this before.” His gaze is alarming and I think that I have said something wrong. I was only trying to be honest with him. I hear him exhale and smile at me.

“Are you still a virgin Faith?” I nod at his question feeling exposed under his intense gaze.

“How can that be, you’re 24?” his reply pisses me off a little, I’m still lying half naked on his bed.

“Well I never planned on staying a virgin. With school, and a dad that betrays you. Then with what Conner tried to do. Well let’s just say, it just never happened.” I snap at him.

“So you will belong to me and only me? See, now I like that plan.” Do I want to belong to Damien yes I do. I want him to erase the memory of what Conner tried to do.

Damien can do that, I know he has the power to replace that scumbags every touch, he can create new memories, ones I actually want to go to sleep to remember. If I only have this once, I want it to be with him.

“Yes, I will belong to you.” my words seem to make his last bit of control snap. He smashes his mouth against mine in a kiss. This is not just a kiss. He is branding me, claiming me as his. When his lips do break away from mine, I'm left panting and breathless.

"I'm not Conner, Faith you say stop, I will stop. Do you trust me?" At his words I realise it's true. I do trust him. I trust him to keep me safe, I trust him to protect me, but most of all I trust him with my heart and my body.

"Yes" I breathe it's the only word I manage. He gets up and starts to take his clothes off. His shirt is the first thing that gets thrown onto the floor, leaving me free to stare at the god-like quality of his chest. He is pure muscle, every muscle is defined and taut, my eyes wander over his tattooed arms, and then down to the v that leads to his… *oh good Lord.*

As my eyes drop, so do his pants. I see his cock, it's beautiful, there's no other way to describe it, standing hard and straight. I snap my eyes up quickly to his. He smirks at me and starts to advance towards me. I let him pull my bra and thong off. His kisses trail up and down my body. I automatically open my legs for him to nestle between them, his fingers find my core and he inserts one inside me and I feel the moisture that now coats his finger. He works it faster, only going deep enough to push against the barrier, I don't know how much more of this I can take, and the pleasure is phenomenal. I feel my body climbing higher, and then when he applies his thumb to my clit I explode crying out, his name on my lips.

"Perfect" he says, He positions himself at my entrance.

"Shit I need to get a condom, hang on" I keep my hold on to him not wanting to let him go

"I'm on the pill, Damien, please." I plead with him I'm ready, I want to feel all of him.

"You will be the only one, I have ever not worn a condom for. I'm clean, are you sure Faith? If we do this, if I feel all of you, I won't give you up again Faith, I can't."

His words melt my heart and I say the first thing that comes to mind.

"Please, Damien." he moans at my words, and starts to push forward. Oh fuck that's tight, I feel myself stretching to accommodate his size. I feel him stop, and then he slowly withdraws before he pushes himself all the way in. I yelp at the sharp pain that runs through me. When he is all the way inside he pauses, and holds himself there letting me adjust. After a moment the pain subsides, and I feel pleasure it burns through my body like a wave, looking up at Damien. "I'm ok now." He nods his head and starts to pull back out and push back in. We start to build a rhythm. When I'm moving my hips to meet each of his thrusts, I feel that climb again. He kisses me again and I float away, wanting to feel every ounce of power he holds in that stunning body. I start to claw at his back wanting him to move faster. I need to reach that peak again. "Faster, please Damien." he hears my words and starts to speed up, but with speed, comes his raw power. Each thrust moves me further up his bed. Clinging to him. As my body climbs I am right on the edge, but something is missing. I don't know what I need. When he looks into my eyes he must see, he places his thumb against the little nub and rubs. "Come for me Faith, right now. I want to feel every part of you over my cock." at his words I detonate around him. I feel him tense inside of me, I feel his warm release deep inside of me. My eyes flutter closed, as I ride the waves until I come back down from heaven.

I wince a little as he pulls out. He rolls to the side and pulls me into him, putting his arm around me, holding me securely to him. He is kissing me, while running his other arm up and down the length of my spine. I soon drift off into a peaceful sleep.

When I wake, the light shining through the windows tells me that I must have slept here all night. I feel the spot at the side of the bed and notice that it's still warm. A pang of disappointment floods me, realising that I'm alone. Stretching out my arms, I get out of bed and I feel the slight sting between my legs. Padding over to the bathroom.

I switch the shower on. I fell in love with this bathroom as soon as I saw it. The walk in shower is all glass it has more jets and heads than any one person really needs. But I bet they do feel heavenly against your skin.

The wall of mirrors that the twin sinks are against is opposite the shower, the room feels light and airy, the tones of cream used in the tiles on the wall, they match some of the creams in the bedroom.

Stepping inside the shower, I feel the warm spray encase my body, the heat from the water, firing out of the jets is cleaning me from head to toe. The only downside is that it is washing away the feel of Damien.

I quickly finish washing, and step out. Wanting to get dried and dressed for the day, I head into the bedroom wanting to find my clothes. I need to check on Cami. I feel like a shit friend. I didn't even check on her last night. What sort of person does that? I dumped her. Basically because I wanted to be with him, oh God what must she think of me especially after everything that happened to her yesterday?

Throwing on some black yoga pants and my white vest top, I sit on the bed, my head starts to ache with everything that has happened in the last 24 hours. What sort of person sleeps with a man that held them captive! We can't have a life together. I don't think I would be ok knowing what he does for a living. With the little bit of information I do know about him, I know that he is dangerous, powerful and feared by most. Thinking back to yesterday when he held Jake against the wall and then he beat him to a pulp. Then told them to get my dad found, I know he will kill him, once his men find him. I am not so bothered about him, its Damien's soul that I worry about, how much darkness can one person live with before they can never come back to the light.

Damien does have good inside of him, I know that he has, I've seen it. I think that's why I am not running. He did let me go and he has been looking after me ever since. When I have needed him he has been there. Watching me, protecting me.

I just don't think, I am what he needs to save his soul. I don't think I have enough strength left to try. The single tear that falls down my cheek, that one tear is the passing of what could have been, if we had met in another life, another time and definitely under different circumstances. I would have been his everything, and I never would have ever doubted him.

I have had enough of this pity party for one now. I decide I need to go and see my girl. I leave the bedroom to go and find Cami's room. I find myself at the foot of an oak spiral stair case that has a floating handrail, it is a sight to behold. I walk up the beautiful staircase and down the long hallway, this is how much of a bad friend I am. I don't even know which room she is in. How pathetic is that.

I knock gently on the first door. Waiting for a reply, I hear nothing so I proceed to the next door further down the hall. Raising my hand to knock again. I pause when I hear the muffled voices from the other side of the room. Quietly listening I recognise Cami's voice straight away and I think the other one is Malc's. Now knowing whom the voices belong to I knock.

The door flings open, and a very angry looking Malc, stands in the doorway. His fists are clenched tight at his sides.

"What." he shouts but then realising that it's me stood in front of him at the door. He lets out an exaggerated breath.

"Sorry Faith."

"It's ok, I just wanted to see if Cami is ok" I tell him, God I feel really awkward just standing here. He nods and steps aside so that I can pass.

I see Cami sat on the couch in the bedroom. She is looking out of the window. Just sat staring she looks fragile.

"Will you give us a minute, please Malc?" I ask him, I want to talk to my friend without a chaperone.

"Of course, I will just be outside Camilla" with that he turns and leaves us to it.

I tentatively make my way over to the couch and sit down beside her. She gives me a glance, and then her tears fall.

"I'm so sorry Cami, I hope they catch my dad and punish him. I really do. Because what he did to you is unforgivable." She nods at my words but does not speak.

"Talk to me Cami, please, is it because of what happened yesterday why you are crying."

She shakes her head, and looks down to her folded hands that rest in her lap.

"Then why are you crying, what's happened?" I beg her to talk to me.

She shakes her head again and I know I am not going to get anything out of her. So I decide to talk about Damien and me. See if she will at least talk about that with me.

"They're going to find him Cami, I promise. But I need to talk to you about something. I spent the night with Damien."

She whips her head around so fast at my words, I think she is going to get whiplash.

"What do you mean you spent the night?" she speaks, I let out a breath, I knew that would get her talking.

"Fine I shall rephrase, I had sex with him and spent the night in his bed."

I can't believe I have just said that out loud, when I close my eyes I can still feel his lips on my skin, his hand on my body, his dick buried deep inside of me. I know it's wrong but I want all of that again.

"Why Faith? Why would you sleep with him? It's because of him that we are stuck in this house. I am afraid to go home Faith, if it's not him wanting you, then it's your father. He is trying to either sell you or kill you. Can't you see how fucked up this is Faith."

What can I say to that? She is right, I know she is, and I love her all the more for her honesty. Even after what she has been through she is brave and calling me out on my bullshit.

"I didn't plan it. It just happened Cami. I was selfish and wanted to forget all about the shit for a minute. I wanted to just be a woman with a man. I wanted to feel

Cami. I have spent the last 6 months feeling dead inside. I wanted him to get rid of every trace of Conner, wherever his hands had been or touched I wanted Damien's to replace them."

"Are you forgetting one little fact, this all started because of him." she shouts at me.

So as calmly as I can manage I reply. The only fact that I am sure of in this whole mess, it was not Damien who caused all this mess.

"No Cami, my father started this!"

She huffs at me when I finish speaking.

"If you really believe that, then you're as crazy as you have been acting."

"Fine, you spit your dummy out. At least he is trying to fix this. Giving you somewhere you can be safe." I get up and turn to walk away not wanting to hear anything else, yes his lines may have been blurry, but his heart was in the right place.

"You think we are safe, what happens when they don't find your dad do you think we will be safe then."

I just manage to catch her sentence as I slam her door behind me and walk past Malc, I need to find Damien, and I want to know what's going on.

Marching back down the stairs, I go in search of him I check the kitchen he's not in there, checked the living room and nothing. I see his office door is ajar and I poke my head around the door. My heart drops when I see him.

He is sat at his desk with his head buried in his hands I can't help it. I go to rush over to him. The scene in front of me tugs at my heart. I place my hand on his shoulder and squeeze it tightly letting him know that I am here for him, if he needs me. He looks up at me, and in that moment I see it right there in his eyes. The pain, worry and fear.

He is broken, just like me.

CHAPTER EIGHT

Damien

I SIT IN the office waiting for a call from Jake, they haven't stopped trying to find him. Malc came back earlier, but I haven't seen him yet, I have been hiding in my office like a coward.

I could not think of a better night's sleep I'd ever had, nothing could beat keeping her wrapped in my arms. When I woke this morning looking at her, I had all these emotions booming around in my chest. I need to keep a clear head, but thinking of last night, the way she felt against me, my dick is already starting to get hard again, and right now I need to focus on finding Darren and keeping her safe.

The ringing of my phone pulls me from my thoughts, seeing Jake's name flash on the screen, I slide my finger across the screen to answer.

“Well, do you have news?” I bark at him, I wanted answers no I needed answers.

“Yeah boss I have news, I’m on my way back now I will tell you as soon as I get there.”

His answer was vague, but I suspected it was because he was driving so I suppose I will have to wait until he gets here.

“Right, see you soon.” I hang up before he has a chance to reply, Jake has only been working with me for the past 5 or so months, he came to me looking for work and I gave him a chance, the only time he has let me down was when her dad got close to her at the apartment, apart from that he has not put a foot wrong and he works well with Malc, and does as he is told. I bury my head in my hands. This situation is getting out of control. I feel a hand on my shoulder gently squeezing. I know who it is before she even speaks.

I have wanted her all morning, it was becoming extremely uncomfortable, the bulge pressing hard against my zip, aching for release. I turn to look at her, I don’t think I have ever seen anything as beautiful, dressed in yoga pants and a tiny vest top, hair drying naturally from the shower, and skin free from make-up, she looks stunning, and that voice inside my head is screaming, she is all mine.

“Are you ok?” she asked me, her voice was quiet, like she was afraid of the answer.

“I’m fine Faith, I assure you, what do you need?”

“When I woke up you were gone and I have questions that need answers.”

“Well then, by all means, ask away.” I tell her, I think in the pit of my stomach, I know what she is going to ask, but it does not make it any easier to swallow, I just want to get this over with.

"Tell me what made you let me go Damien, I need to understand please." There it was this is the third time she has asked, there really is no getting away from it now.

She waits patiently for me to speak. I pull her down to sit on my lap, at least if I am going to tell her my darkest secrets I want her close. It may be the last time that she lets me hold her and if it is, I am going to make sure I hold her tight because I will fight to my last breath to keep hold of her.

"I had a sister Bella, she was so sweet and pure, like my little shadow, followed me everywhere. One summer I went away on business for my father and I did not see her or speak to her much over the coming months. I assumed it was because she was young and busy enjoying going out with her friends. Little did I know that my family had been torn apart by lies and deceit and hatred. I came home to find that my mother had left my father and that my sister was gone. He said that there was nothing I could do, he had sold her so that he could have the trade of drugs in London, she was part of the deal, he wouldn't tell me where she was. Every day for over a week I asked him, no begged him to tell me where Bella was and everyday he laughed at me."

I start to feel the tears burning in my eyes, why was it so hard to talk about this. I could feel my chest getting tighter as I continued to speak about Bella, the heart she had was beautiful inside and out she never got involved with the family business, she just wanted to go to school graduate and be with her friends.

"In the end I locked him in a room and beat him, until he gave me the name of the man that had her, I never thought that I would hate my father Faith, so I do know what you are going through. Malc and I found the guy that had her. He was still in London. I made the decision then, that I was going to get her back."

I don't think I can tell her anymore, I look up to see that her eyes are full, she brings her hand up to my cheek and holds me, it is the most tender of touches but it's what I need right in this moment, I take from her strength.

"We went to get her, killed every one in that house searching for her, I didn't care, I was like a man possessed looking for my baby sister, I walked into that hole of a room where they had her, she was beaten to a pulp and lay in a pool of her own blood. I was too late I could not save her Faith."

I heard her intake of breath when I softly spoke the last words, but that's only half of the story.

She cradled me close pulling me right into her chest; I wrapped both of my arms around her needing her to accept all of me.

"You don't have to tell me the rest Damien, I can see it's tearing you apart talking about it." Her voice was soothing and comforted me in a way I had never felt before.

I lift my head from her chest looking into her eyes I saw nothing but acceptance in them whether it was for the man or the crime I'm not sure. Only time will tell, what I can say is that while I was looking in her eyes the need in me rose. I need to feel every part of her make sure she is still here with me. Bringing my hand up to the back of her neck I pull her down to me and placed an urgent kiss against her lips it was hot and heavy, I bite at her bottom lip so that I could gain access to her mouth I need to explore every part of her. She opened for me with a moan when I tugged at it a second time, she came back and matched my movements perfectly her hands come up and fist into my shirt pulling me closer to her, this kiss was not going to be enough my cock ached and the need to be inside of her was going to consume me. I turned her so that she now straddled me, I wanted to feel her warm core rubbing up against me but didn't have time for foreplay I wanted to be buried deep inside of her, trailing my kisses down her neck, I was so hard. "Baby I need to fuck you right now." I carried on kissing down her neck, over the swell of her breast, she nodded and my reply was not words it was actions. I lifted her up and spun her round she was now stood with her back to my chest, she was a sight to behold dirty blonde hair hanging loose, tight yoga pants fit like a glove over the curve of her arse.

"I am going to bend you over my desk and fuck you now Faith, I am going to make you scream my name as I make you cum." She moaned and nodded and it was the most fucking amazing sound I have ever heard, I slowly pulled at her pants tugging them down her thighs to her knees, she has her legs slightly parted as if her instinct guided her. Oh fuck she has no knickers on. Shit I nearly cum just from looking at her bare arse exposed to me. I give it a gentle slap. "I like you bent over my desk." I tugged at my trousers as quickly as I could, and got them down around my ankles. I didn't care, I gripped hold of my cock and started to rub it in her wetness, her liquid coated my dick making it nice and wet. She moaned when my tip brushed against her clit. I pulled back to start the torture all over again, I can smell the tang of her wetness, taste it on the tip of my tongue and hell if it doesn't make me ache to be inside of her. I don't think I can hold on much longer.

Jesus. I'm not even inside her and I want to cum like some horny fucking teenager.

"Please, I need you inside me."

Her words where my undoing, I line myself up and thrust all the way inside of her. I felt her warm heat wrap around me. She is so fucking tight. I love it knowing that she is mine and only mine. That caveman instinct inside of me comes to life whenever I'm near her. I pull back slowly and push forward again harder this time sending her further across my desk. I grip hold of her hips and pull her back to me hard. She moans my name and it drives me fucking crazy. I thrust inside of her again, wanting to feel her let go again, knowing that I control her pleasure. I slap her arse again and look at the nice pink mark that is now glowing. It covers her backside. I pump my hips faster now, wanting to feel that sweet release knowing that it is Faith bringing it to me. I don't think I will ever get enough of her. I feel her insides tighten as my speed increases, a few faster, deep strokes will send me over the edge. I hear her moaning, but it's not enough, I needed her to scream out my name. I don't care who hears I want everyone to know she is mine. That I am doing this to her, making her body responds to mine. I place my fingers on her clit and rub, then gently I pinch the sensitive bundle of nerves and I hear her screaming out my name. Her pussy clamps hard around my dick as she falls over the edge. Every muscle in her body is rigid as she rides her climax. As she comes down, I feel the tightness of my balls as they pull up tight and I feel pulse after pulse of my release empty inside of her. I fall forward and rest my cheek against her back utterly spent my heaving chest feels heavy and my body now spent.

"Wow, that was just… wow… I have no words" her words bring a smile to my face, I pull myself up off of her back, pulling out I pull my trousers back up and tuck myself away, bending down I pull Faith's yoga pants back up and cover her up. When she leans up off the desk she spins around to face me.

"Now that you have that out of you system, do you want to tell me the rest of the story?" it has to come out so why not now, the knocking at the door pulls my attention from Faith.

"Yes" I shout, the door opens and in walks Jake.

"Sir, can we talk?" I look over to Faith, not wanting her to hear what was going to be said just yet.

"Faith will you please give us a minute." Fuck I even ask her to do things not demand like I do with everyone else.

She just nods her head and makes her way out of the office closing the door behind her.

I sit down in my chair and just look at him, there was something that just does not quite sit right. I'm not sure what it is but I have this gut feeling. When they say don't judge a book by its cover, well that's all I had to go off Jake he had no background, no history and no family or so the background check I had done on him revealed.

He sits down opposite me and looked directly at me he didn't seem nervous or scared to be in my presence so I just sit and wait for him to spill the information that he has gathered so far.

"He is hiding Sir." Well no shit Sherlock I thought to myself as If I didn't already know that.

"That much I had pretty much worked out for myself Jake, do you have anything important to tell me or not." I tell him wanting him to just come right out and say it, why do people do that beat around the bush to make a point, it really does tick me off I have better things to do with my time.

"Of course sir, we tracked him down to a hotel in the city where he is staying but he has bodyguards with him so we could not get to him, so Malc came back here and I was to watch which is what I did sir. After a couple of hours a man left his hotel with a large case, from what I have been able to gather is that he has paid for protection," Right well that's not too bad I knew he would go into hiding it was pretty obvious, so why the importance that's what I don't get I need him to finish explaining it too me right now

"Sir he has no money to pay for protection, he has promised them something when all this has blown over." I was getting that feeling again in the pit of my stomach that my world was going to fall from under my feet.

"What has he promised them in return for protection Jake." His head dropped down to his chest and I knew by looking at him that I was not going to like the answer one little bit.

"Faith" he said. With that I roar at him to get the fuck out.

I shout for the one man I need.

"MALC."

Chapter Nine

Faith

I HEAR HIM shouting Malc's name and I run back towards his office. What the fuck has Jake said to him, to cause him to want Malc right at this moment.

I don't stop to knock, I just burst through his office door, and stop right in front of him, the amber liquid was sliding effortlessly down his throat, his head was tipped right back as he finished his drink, he slammed the glass down so hard on his desk I thought it was going to smash.

"What happened?" I ask him as his head snapped up to me as if he had only just realised I was there.

"Just leave it Faith, go and wait for me in the living room I will be in soon." How dare he just order me out who the fuck does he think he is just because we have fucked twice does not give him the power to rule me, hell no!

"I only came to see what was going on, I don't need a fucking lecture you arsehole." Rage runs through me at this point and I just want to slap him, across that face, gone is the man who 30 minutes ago had me bent over this desk making me scream for a whole other reason and in his place is the arrogant, self-assured prick of a boss who has to control every little detail of what is going on around him.

"I told you to leave Faith. This does not concern you. It's my fucking business not yours." he snaps at me and I feel like a child being told off, to say my mood was really becoming sour was an understatement.

"You know what fine, have it your way I will go."

I turn around walking back the way I came in, just *who the hell does he think he is*? The arrogant arse, he wants me to go, fine! That's what I will do. I rush down the hall and pass the living room coming to his bedroom. Stepping inside I slam the door behind me, I don't care if I am heard, I want to stomp, scream and throw something heavy, preferably at his head. But he hasn't followed me so I will just have to settle for the wall.

Pulling my bag out of his walk in wardrobe, I stomp around some more pulling my few items of clothes that I brought with me and stuffing them into the bag I don't care if they are folded or not. I want out of this house.

Zipping up the bag I grab my jacket and bag and set off, the only aim in my head is to get out of this house.

I walk out of the door from the bedroom and head towards the front door of this beautiful house, the natural creams and brown colours that line all the walls make it clean and warm and inviting I wonder who decorated this house was it a ex or a designer or a family member. It just goes to show I hardly know anything about him, the only thing I am certain of is my body's reaction to his kisses and touches. They make me feel alive something, I did not even realise that I was missing from my life how can one person live everyday but not feel alive, I don't think I will ever not crave his touch.

I see the door ahead of me and I walk as quickly as I can, when I reach it I see that no one has come looking for me. Pulling open the door I get outside, just as I walk away, I feel the hand clamp around my arm spinning me back around, but it's not who I expected it to be, "Malc" I breath slightly scared and relieved at the same time.

"Where do you think you're going Faith, you know you can't be out here it's not safe." His words are a warning but they show that he cares as well.

"Well I'm not staying in there, you should have heard how he spoke to me, and I am not some drone he can order about."

I realise I do not want to be someone he orders about, damn feelings always stirring up trouble where there should be none, after all if it wasn't for Damien then I would be at the hands of my father suffering God knows what. "Just give him time to sort his shit out Faith." I do like Malc's voice it has a lovely low tone to it, the accent did make him sound sexy and gruff but it was nothing compared to Damien's, his silky voice makes my insides squirm.

"What does he expect me to do? Just stand there while he dictates to me. That just isn't going to happen." As the anger flares up again, it was also embarrassment that I was feeling, the way he had spoken to me like that. That is what really had me running, I know deep down that I do not want to leave, but I'm making a stand, damn it.

"I can't let you leave you know that, don't make me manhandle you, I've done it before I will do it again little one, I don't answer to you, he gives me my orders and I listen and follow." I shrink back a little at the memory of being taken, all that I had come to endure due to my father's actions still burned deep, but to come face to face with the man who had actually taken me. I didn't know what to feel. On one hand I should run kicking and screaming but on the other, the few times that I had seen him since, he has not hurt me. The way he saved my best friend and has looked after her since, has me wondering about the man he is, I know it's wrong to push him, but I can't help the snarky comment that leaves my mouth.

"Like a lap dog you mean," I knew the instant my eyes met his I had pushed him too far, His hands fisted at his sides so quick, I almost missed it, but with my next breath, I was hoisted up over his shoulder his arm clamped around my legs holding them securely to him. He lowered his other arm and picked up my bag and walked back into the house. Well this can't get any worse, I thought to myself I started smacking his back with my closed fists.

"Put me down you big oaf" I scream, something that isn't that easy when you are dangling upside down. I can feel the blood rushing to my head as he took his giant strides, the man was solid my stomach hurt from where is shoulder blade was digging in. His arms got tighter around my legs to combat my punches and jerky movements, he chuckled at me and carried on walking into the hall of the house all the while I was screaming, blue bloody murder.

He carries on walking through the house towards the door of Damien's bedroom.

"Malcolm! Put her down now!" Oh God. Cami's voice, the tone she used with him sends shivers down my spine he halts suddenly and spins round to look at her.

"I was told to take her back to her room, so that's what I am doing Camilla." His tone does not sound amused so he opens the door to Damien's room and strides right inside.

I know my girl she has this. She will fight tooth and nail for me. Even if she does not like me so much right now, our conversation before had not ended too well.

"You put her down right now, or else." she paused for a moment, waiting for him to answer. "Malc please put her down." I feel his body relax under me and he gives into her plea. He places me on the ground holding me steady whilst Cami comes rushing over to me, as she reaches me I fall into her embrace.

"Thank you," she whispered to Malc. He just nods at her then turns and walks away. Cami walks me back further into Damien's bedroom. Not knowing where to look I was so embarrassed, thinking about the few people that had witnessed me being carried though the house kicking and screaming like a toddler having a hissy fit. It is not a high point of my life so far.

"What happened Faith?" I did everything I could not to meet her gaze but she waited patiently for me to answer. We are standing at the foot of the bed her arms are holding on to me.

"He told me to leave so I did. Then that big brute brought me back, the rest you know." I did not mean to snap at Cami really I didn't, it's my humiliation that is causing this reaction.

"Are you finished now?" she asks me, so I just nod what more could I do.

"So what happened then and I want the proper version not the spit your dummy out version." I nod looking at her.

"He shouted at me, told me to get out, that it was not my business."

"And was it your business what they were discussing." I shake my head

"He shouted for Malc, and I went running in like a woman possessed." I admitted she nods at me, she knows what I am like if someone shouts at me I am going to shout back that's just me.

"So what you're saying to me, is that you barged into whatever was happening, and jumped the gun as normal."

I nodded again feeling like an idiot,

"Hang on before, you could not stand him, hated everything he stood for, what has changed?" I question her, she really does not seem that surprised

"Look I'm not saying that I agree with everything he has done but he is keeping you safe Faith, just listen to him and do as he says." she knows something I could see it in her eyes, she was trying to placate me, I hate it when she pulls the mother routine on me.

"What is it Cami what do you know, tell me please?"

"Look it's not for me to say, just wait for him to come and tell you, I am not really supposed to know." I was getting frustrated with her lack of explanation.

"You tell me what you know Cami now! Don't you dare keep things from me just who do you think you are."

Her eyes heated and I could feel the anger radiating off her, I feel the sharp slap across my cheek, my face begins to burn, I hiss through my teeth when I realise what the fuck she has just done, I stand ready to slap her back when I am pulled away from behind.

"I can't let you do that Faith." it was Malc again why the fuck is he even in here.

"This has nothing to do with you, lap dog. Now let go of me." I scream struggling against his hold.

"It has everything to do with me…." Cami cut him off by giving him a pointed look and proceeding to get right in my face.

"He is going to sell you again, you silly girl for once in your life listen to people who want to help you."

I go lax and stopped fighting, oh God no I can't do this again. What the fuck has gone on now? Malc lets me go, I slump to the floor burying my head in my hands.

"Faith." I don't even look up when Damien says my name I am drained emotionally I have nothing left to give so I cry. I let it all out. The hate. The pain. The loss.

"Leave us," I hear him say to them and I hear the click of the door closing as they leave.

I feel him pick me up off the floor and gently lay me down on the bed, he lies down next to me and pulls me in close. Feeling his arms wrapped around me brings me back from the edge of my meltdown. I open my eyes and look around the room, so glad that it is just Damien and I. I let myself relax into his embrace.

“Why is he still doing this?” I whisper into the room not really caring if I get a response or not. I just want to speak the words it makes it real. I know then that it’s not something I have imagined. It’s something I am living and it’s a hell that I don’t want to live. But without this hell, I would not have Damien wrapped around me right now holding me, keeping me safe, protecting me.

“I won’t let him have you Faith, you are my light I can’t have him try to put you out.”

At his words I sob that little bit harder, not knowing what to say, so I mumble the only thing that feels right at that moment.

“Find him and kill him please.”

“I will, he won’t ever hurt you again baby,”

I drift off into a restless sleep, I know as soon as I see Conner’s face that I am dreaming again, it starts the same way as always, last night I didn’t have the dream, I don’t see Damien, he doesn’t appear. This dream is different. My dad is there and he is laughing at me telling me that he owns me, I am his to do as he sees fit, and he brought me into this world so he has the power to take me out of it.

I startle myself awake with his lingering words in my mind. Gasping I clutch my chest tightly trying to calm my erratic beating heart.

“Faith what’s the matter are you ok?” I hear his voice and I start to nod, I feel the need to pull him close. So I lie back down taking deeper breaths to try and calm myself down.

“Ssh its ok, it was only a dream.” He says to me while running his fingers gently though my hair, he places a gentle kiss against my forehead and it's what I need to send me back to sleep.

My eyes blink against the bright morning light and I feel something pressed up against my back, that's when I realise where I am and who is next to me and I feel relieved that he is still here with me. He held me all night, chased away the nightmare and not once did he let me go.

"Morning, are you ok?" he says. Pressing himself closer to me. I smile to myself, before answering him.

"Morning" I say as his hand trails down the front of my body, my breath catches in my throat, he presses light kisses to my ear, and I feel the length of him pressing into the base of my back. I turn to face him and seeing the look in his eyes, I know exactly what I need.

"Make me forget Damien," I say with lust filled eyes, at my words he does just that and more.

Chapter Ten

Damien

AFTER MY SHOWER, I walk back into the bedroom. In the closet I notice that all of her things are still packed and I don't like it, I want her stuff next to mine it's where it belongs, I knew yesterday after the way I spoke to her she was pissed off with me, she was only running scared.

I nearly burst out laughing when I saw that Malc had her over his shoulder, arms flailing around in the air trying to hurt his back.

Dressed in my white shirt, black trousers and my favourite black tie, in the bedroom she is sat at my dresser putting her hair up, I love it when she wears it down, it cascades around her shoulders weaving my fingers through and grasping hold tightly in the throes of…. Shit I need to stop that train of thought or we will be having round two and round one was heavenly, I could get used to waking up with her in my arms.

"We still need to talk about yesterday," I say to her, noting her eyes widen in the mirror as she looks back at me.

"I know" she all but whispered

"We know where he is, but we can't get near him yet, he has bodyguards surrounding him."

"What did Cami mean yesterday, she said he was going to sell me again?"

"Right I will tell you what we know, I didn't want to tell you yesterday in front of everyone because I didn't want you getting upset." She just nods her head in understanding. So I continue with our conversation, I know she has a right to know but is it so bad to want to protect her from it all.

"What we think we know from Jake, is that he has no money to pay for protection so he used the only thing he could use, and that's you. I won't let him near you Faith do you understand you are mine, not his, MINE!" I growl the last bit out the caveman instincts kicking in to provide and protect, it's a strange feeling to live with, when you have gone so long being told that emotion is weak and it will destroy you.

"I hate him for what he is trying to do to me, I promise I won't try to run again, I got scared with everything that has been going on. When you shouted at me in your office, I felt like a child being told off, it was humiliating."

I had known how she felt but at the time my anger was high. I didn't want her to see. I thought by getting her out, where she could not hear, it would be better for her sanity.

"I am sorry Faith I just wanted to protect you, I did not mean to snap but I had just found out myself and the thought of anybody else but me touching you is unthinkable." I was honest with my words no point hiding them now.

"I know and I am sorry too for running, think I owe Malc and Cami an apology too, I kind of called Malc a lapdog," she giggled the last part of her sentence, it was a beautiful sound, something I want to hear a lot more of in the future.

"Right come on let's go and get some breakfast shall we, you need to keep your strength up."

I pull her up from the dresser and lead her out of the bedroom all the while holding her hand.

In the kitchen I see Malc, Cami, and Jake all sat around my huge oak table laughing amongst themselves, it's been so long since laughter has graced this house, the morning sunshine that streams in through the bi-folding doors, it brightens the entire kitchen.

Sitting at the table, I see that the cook has placed a great variety of food down, to accommodate every pallet, Faith takes the seat at my side, and yeah I like her beside me.

"Right we need to get down to business." Malc raises his brow to me wondering why I would talk with the ladies around, he has a point normally I wouldn't but the ladies are very much involved and need to know what they can and cannot do.

"Do we have updates on Darren?" I aim my question to Malc.

"Boss things are pretty much the same, he has not left unescorted from the hotel." he keeps his answer polite but I can see the tension in his eyes, I need to find out what is going on with my friend.

First I need to deal with this it is taking its toll and I want it done with now I want *moya lyubov* to be safe, shit where did that come from I have not spoken Russian since I was at home with my father, it was his native language and he spoke it often, I have never been to Russia, my dad chose to stay here, when he met my mother and they fell in love, he started the business with Anton at his side and they never went back. I heard him and my mother talking on many a night as to why he stayed but they never spoke of it in front of me.

Anton is Malc's dad so we grew up together; we have been with each other since the beginning.

I swore that I would never represent anything that father of mine stood for, but the words sound right, she is my love and I will do anything to keep her.

"Right, Jake I want you to go and watch the hotel again count how many keepers he has with him, then report back to me later on. Then we will need to form a plan to take him. I want him finished. Malc call Anton and have him bring my mother here I want everyone on lockdown, plus we will need his certain skill set for what I have in mind." Anton was a master at getting into anywhere, he can slip in and slip out, without being detected. He has a lot of people that owe him favours, he can also find out more information on a person than any background check ever could.

"Right Boss no problem." Jake got up to leave, to do his job. I may have given him a black eye and a busted lip and brushed what he did under the carpet for now, but there is just something about him that does not sit well with me.

"Right ladies would you mind giving Malc and me a minute please I have a couple of things we need to discuss." They both nod, but I don't miss the look that Cami gives Malc it's a don't you dare look, they both get up to leave and I wrap my arm around Faith and crush my lips to her mouth, tracing the seam of her lips she opens without any hesitation, I devour her mouth, I love the way she tastes it's sweet like cotton candy, realising we are not alone I begrudgingly release her, she smiles at me and it strikes me right in my core how magnificent she truly is for someone with so much crap on her plate she still gives you her all.

"If you want to make use of the gardens to the back of the house, or the pool please feel free ladies and we will come and find you both shortly." They both leave the room and I wonder if their friendship will survive this.

I turn and sit back down looking at my friend wanting to know what his haunting him.

"What is going on my friend, you're unfocused with the task at hand."

He rubbed his hand across his chin, before looking straight at me

"Women, I don't understand them, they are a puzzle, so hot and cold." Ha well who would have thought it was a woman, Malc is not a man that forms attachments easily and he certainly does not trust quickly, I know who this is about but I want to hear it from him.

"So who is the lucky lady that is confusing you my friend?"

"Camilla" his only word that escapes from his mouth.

"So what has happened then?" I hold back my snigger knowing exactly what he is going through.

"I don't know, damn woman is hot one minute and cold the next, it's driving me mad, how the hell did you get Faith to be ok with all of this." Huh is that what he thinks that I have all my ducks in a row where my girl is concerned, huh. Far fucking from it.

"I don't think she will ever be ok with this life Malc. I have to show her that no matter what happens or what life brings to us I will never waver, my feelings will never falter," I don't think I even believe the words that are coming out of my mouth, will she ever be ok with this life, my life.

"I don't know what to do she frustrates the hell out of me Damien."

"Just give her time Malc it's all you can do."

"Thanks man I appreciate it. I will try to get on top of it."

I take his words as his hint that he does not want to talk anymore about it and uses it to direct the conversation towards my mother and Anton.

"Make sure you phone Anton as soon as we are done here." And with that he knows it's back to business.

"Yeah I will do Boss, what do you want me to say over the phone to them?" he asks and it's then I realise my mother has not got a clue about Faith or what I did or what I am doing, shit I think to myself how the hell is this going to play out, she won't have a go in front of anyone, she would not show me up like that, but I can be damn well sure she is going to bend my ear in private, I do want her to know about her, I want my mother to like her.

"Just tell them that I need them up here for a couple of days, urgently!"

"Yes boss, you know she is going to kick your arse when she finds out, don't you?" I grumble at his words knowing they're bloody true, 30 years old and I would stand there while she did it to. She understands that in the business I am at the head of the table in control of what happens with this family. But that does not mean I would ever disrespect my mother, she understands the things I did and the reasons why, even if she did not like the way I did them.

"I know, now get it done and tell the staff to have rooms prepared for their visit." I walk out of the kitchen noting that all the food has been cleaned up the sides all wiped clean and nothing out of place. The staff do anticipate my needs without any fuss or delay.

I come to a stop in my office looking out of the window I see her sat in the garden, Cami is with her and they seem to be talking about what, I do not know. The sun is shining down on her and when she turns to look towards the house, as if sensing someone is watching, it takes my breath away I try to turn away but she holds me captive for a few more seconds.

I spend the next couple of hours in the office looking into the businesses that I have lent money too, seeing how they are doing financially, if any seem to be falling behind they need to be given a call, if that fails well then it's a visit.

There are a couple of small companies that need a little extra attention but nothing too big, Malc and Jake should be able to sort it out. I won't be letting Faith out of my sight any time soon. Normally I would go with them but she takes precedence.

I took over from my father after I had killed him, he had run it into the ground. I don't deal in women or drugs, only money and guns. I know, who am I, to take the moral high ground, when what I do is still illegal, but there is a legacy at stake, my family name is well renowned, I don't think I could ever leave this life, I may not have wanted it to begin with. But I won't ever walk away. My name commands respect wherever I go, people bend over backwards to help me Damien Volkov, I lead they follow, if they don't follow I make them it's that simple.

I leave the office and hear the girls in the living room talking I walk in and see them both sat on the huge corner sofa, It dominates the space but with the size of the room it needs to, the only thing that takes away from it is the inglenook fire that I have on the main wall, the hardwood floors are covered in rugs. I do like the creams and reds and browns that run all through this house, the designer did capture everything I wanted in a home, a place where I can raise children, family and friends to always feel free to visit and always feel welcome.

"Are you two ok?" I ask wondering if they need anything.

"We are fine thank you just catching up," at her words they both giggle and I shake my head and turn back to head out of the room, women and their gossip, I'm glad they can laugh about this and are talking again, I am not sure on the ins and outs of their relationship but they seem close.

The kitchen is a hive of activity as the cook prepares for our evening meal, I can't wait for the night to fall to say our goodnights and to be back with her in my arms and my bed, I need to feel her skin against mine, watch over her while she sleeps cradled in my arms, show her how she is *moi prekrasnye svet.* My beautiful light.

Because without her the darkness would fill me, with her by my side I can see the light and I want to go towards the light. Only she can chase the demons away.

Chapter Eleven

Jake

I SIT IN the black SUV outside the hotel waiting for the right time to go in, I have sat here in this car for the past two days watching, waiting. I crack my knuckles, bored of the hanging around, I mean how long does it take for a hooker to leave. It can't take that long for an ugly fuck like him to blow his load.

What feels like hours later I see the two bit tramp walk out escorted by one of his guards. I step out of the car and stroll across the road to the hotel.

At the doors I see the body builder guy stood there eyeing me up, he has at least double the muscle I have but that does not faze me in the slightest.

"How can I help?" He asks me in a bored tone.

"I'm here to see Mr. Young he is expecting me." I can see him look at me to gauge if I am telling the truth, he talks into some earpiece and a second or two later he is buzzing me up to the suite where he is staying.

Walking into the suite it looks like any other rich hotel, all fancy and overly done, fashionable sofas and a flat screen TV, stepping further inside he greets me "Mr. Masters, what a pleasure to finally meet you." I return the offered hand and give it a firm shake. I release my grip and he directs me to the couch to take a seat. I just want to get this over with I have to make sure I am only gone a certain amount of time, I don't want Damien becoming suspicious just yet I need to set my trap playing both sides of the game. If I want my revenge then I have to play it right. I will get to see the life drain from Damien, as he watches me fuck his girl, knowing he won't be able to help her this time. I will make right what happened, and no one will see it coming but me.

"The pleasure is all mine, I trust the guards are to your liking, keeping you safe." I respond politely as possible.

"And how is the payment doing? Well I hope." See now we get down to business.

"Faith is fine don't you worry about her, once we kill Damien I will keep my payment and your debts will be paid."

"Just how are we supposed to lure him," he asks me "Well we will have to take away the one thing he wants won't we."

His chuckle grates on me "Yes we will." He states

"So you will be waiting at the warehouse for him in two days, I will put the idea that the girls need to go shopping or some bullshit and I will offer to escort them, you will then phone and say that you have her and he is to meet you at the warehouse at a certain time to which we both will lay in wait for him to come." That's just the plan to get him there, what he does not know is the plans I have when he gets there.

"Ok tell me when you have the girls and I will make the call to him." Pleasantries over I see, I stand to make my way out of the hotel turning to him so I can say my final piece.

"You don't follow through, it will be you at that warehouse and protection disappears, understand." He nods his head furiously at me and with that I make my way down stairs back to the car. Time to give Damien a few crumbs.

I sit in the car thinking back to how all this started, I did not know about my father, or where I came from until my mum died, don't feel sorry for me she was a junkie who deserved that overdose. That's when I found the letters from my father addressed to my mother telling her how sorry he was that he could not be with her but he was already married and had a son. So I packed what stuff I had left and went to find him I was 19 years old at the time and travelled from York down to London with the last bit of money I had.

The man I called father never turned me away instead he welcomed me with open arms, he and his wife and son gave me a place to stay, food, clothes and got me a job in the local warehouse, packing up goods for delivery. As the months went by I started to open up to them and they listened, we even went on holiday a couple of times, then my brother went and got involved with the wrong crowd and he changed. He didn't let me hang around with him anymore he said he was protecting me, that he did not want me in this life with him.

I caught him one night with a girl up against the wall at the side of the club where he used to go, she was screaming at him to stop that she did not want it, but by this time he had his hands around her throat squeezing the life from her eyes, as he continued to pump in and out of her.

I watched at first, amazed that he had this raw power over another person, taking away her choice and enjoying it. I found myself growing hard whilst I watched him fucking her. Her tear stained cheeks and her red rimmed eyes, turning me on even more. I unzipped my jeans and released my cock and started fisting my cock pleasuring myself, whilst I watched my brother raping her, when her eyes locked on mine and she mouthed for me to help her, I lost it and came into my hand with a grunt.

I never found satisfaction any other way than either watching Conner or joining in with his games.

Nobody knew but us, we kept it hidden from everyone, then they took Faith and Conner was infatuated with her. Those few weeks they had her he would come home and talk non-stop about her saying how he was going to enjoy it when he fucked every hole she had. Something had happened and he found himself alone looking after Faith, she is beautiful I will say that, Damien had been absent for nearly a week only checking in via phone so Conner had told me that he had it all planned out, he was going to start the day like any other, let her have her food and shower, take her back to her room let her have her last meal. Then he would take her. He had it all planned, he was going to say that she tried to escape and he caught her so she fought back and he killed her. His words were and I quote, *"I'm going to enjoy breaking every hole she has, pumping my seed into her as she takes her last breath."*

He never came home that night and when I went to the address he had given me the next day, I saw my brother stripped naked and strung up, his dick was on the floor at the side of him and the word rapist cut deep into the skin of his chest, his eyes had been removed along with his tongue, each finger was cut off, symbolizing every part of a man that could pleasure or look upon a woman had been removed.

I left him there. I couldn't look at the sight any longer, it was then I decided that I would make whoever did this pay and it could only be one of two people Damien or Malc, I just had to find my way in.

I had stalked them for a couple of weeks waiting for my chance to get an introduction and it came when Malc walked into the restaurant I was eating in, I looked like hell and he bought it hook, line and sinker. I had no connection to Conner so when they did background checks nothing came up, I was good to be brought into the family.

I was cleaned up given new clothes and a room at the house. It was clear to see he was obsessed by the girl only he and Malc got near her at first watching her every move making sure her dad didn't get to her. He had us looking for him every day checking all the information we could get hold of. The Internet had vast knowledge on almost everybody and it was easy enough to hack in to cameras at airports and get passenger lists. Then after nearly six months of plotting and watching I got a hit he was on a plane heading back for London Gatwick. When he landed I checked the picture to make sure that it was him, then I followed him to the little shack of a flat that he went to. Then I called it into Malc.

I set off back to the house after watching that damn hotel a little longer, I had to make it real when I reported back to Damien that he was still there, and that people went in and out to him, but he never left unattended.

It was sheer dumb luck that he turned up at her flat it was only the third time I had been made to watch her, she had been out with her friend but I left them further up the street so I could park without being seen, that's when I saw him enter her building, I did not go in after him, I waited and watched as the girls went into the building, so I made the call to Malc to let him know that her dad was there he said they would be there in five, so I waited at the bottom of the stairwell for them to arrive.

He gave me a black eye and a fucking busted lip for not coming in to help as soon as I realised it was Darren.

It was worth it though to know how much she means to him, so I played along like the happy lackey, waiting for my opportunity to talk to her dad, after we arrived at the house he sent us looking for him, I drove back to the flat he was staying in and rang his phone.

When he answered the conversation was tense at first like he did not believe that I wanted Damien dead for what he had done to my brother, after I explained that I would get him the protection he needed and where to go. I told him that I wanted Faith as payment, and he agreed the arsehole, did he not realise I was going to do everything to her that my brother wanted to do. I will do it different though, I will strip him naked, string him up and only leaving his eyes, so that he can watch as I fuck her taking what she will not give, and as his eyes finally close and he takes his last defining breath, I will finally spill my seed deep inside of her as I slit her pretty little fucking throat.

Arriving at the house I notice it's all smiles the family is sat in the kitchen eating dinner I step through the doors and plaster a smile on my face.

Damien looks up at me and nods what a fucking dick. I am going to enjoy this kill more than all the others.

"Anything to report?" Damien asks me as I sit down at the table,

Smiling as best I can but not to appear fake. "Just the same boss he does not leave, unless guarded. The total number of bodyguards he has is four so that should be easy enough to take down when Anton gets here," of course I know all this, I'm the one that hired all the bodyguards.

"That's great Jake, now that we have that information we can plan when we are going to take them down and retrieve Darren" Malc and me both nod at him.

Tucking into my meal I eat up, I only managed a sandwich at lunch. The conversation runs smoothly around the table the worries seem to fade into the background for now.

Leaving the table I say my goodnights and make my way to the room I sleep in, getting undressed and into bed so I can play out all the delicious things I am going to do to Faith to make her scream with pain, I hope she struggles, I like it when they are feisty and you get to beat compliance into them first. I grip hold of my now rock hard cock pulling it back slowly and gripping hold of my balls tightly, I squeeze them while working myself faster, I cum onto my tummy savouring the image in my head, of her blood spilling from her throat while my cock spurts inside of her.

The time is drawing near to take action.

I will kill Damien and fuck and kill Faith.

With that last thought, I fall into a peaceful sleep counting down the days until my revenge is complete.

Chapter Twelve

Faith

I SPENT MOST of the day yesterday with Cami and we seem to be back on track, she might not like the fact that I'm sleeping with Damien, but there really is nothing she can do about it.

She opened up and gave me a little information on what is going on with her and Malc. She has feelings for him; I can see it written all over her face. She is trying to play it off as a sexual attraction but I could see it was more.

Malc wants her to be with him but she keeps fighting him saying that she won't ever be in this life. That when all of this is over she is going back to her apartment and getting on with her life but apparently that didn't go down too well with Malc. I can't say I blame her. I have the same fear inside of me, but I crave Damien's touch, he does things to my body I didn't realise were possible, and the way he makes me feel? Well, I'm addicted. How the hell am I supposed to walk away from something like that?

Thinking back to last night and first thing this morning I have never felt so loved, so cherished. He worships me, my body and soul with every touch and kiss.

Is it wrong to want to keep him in my life? Probably. Even if how we did meet was screwed up, he is proving himself now keeping me safe, keeping Cami safe? Yes, still probably, but he is a protector, my protector. Hell, he's even having his mother brought here so she is safe. That does not seem like the actions of a mad man with the need to kill.

He told me before he left the bedroom this morning, that his mum Lily and Anton would arrive at around 11am, I am nervous the only parents I have ever met is my own and well look how that turned out, my mother does not even care that I am gone as long as she is kept in the latest fashion with the nicest jewellery, and a different gardener each week she is just fine. That's why I called Cami at the hospital because if I would have thought for a minute that my mum would have dropped my dad and come to my aid, I would have called her but I know she wouldn't do that for me.

Don't get me wrong, in her own way she cares, I was always in the best of everything, even at boarding school I was sent all the latest clothes and shoes, mobile phones.

All a child ever wants is true affection, and to know they are loved, not to be bought. So as the years passed we grew more distant. I can't even remember the last time I spoke to my mother. I think that's why I'm so nervous, never having known true affection maybe it's what I crave now. Will I always seek approval?

I'm sitting in the office with Damien when I hear voices coming from the hall, this is it then. Time to meet his Mum. I'm so nervous. What if she asks how we met or how long I have known him? What do I say? Do I lie or tell the truth? I can feel the panic building so I take a deep breath to try and calm myself. Damien looks up at me sensing my discomfort.

"You ok baby?" he asks me, his voice is soft I can see the concern written all over his face.

"What if she asks how we met?" taking a deep breath I rush out my words, making sure I get them all out. I drop my head, too scared to look in his eyes, worried what I might see in them.

"It's fine, I will talk to her, she won't ask" I don't question him any further. There would not be much point getting into an argument with them right down the hall. So I try to think positive thoughts, it's going to be fine I repeat to myself over and over.

Damien stands and walks over to me, he takes a hold of my clammy hand. It's a strange feeling when you have never had it before, his warm fingers clasp around mine and he pulls me along with him.

Standing there in the hallway, I see a beautiful woman who has just released Malc from a hug. Wow! She is stunning. I would say she doesn't look a day over fifty, even though Damien already said she was sixty, three months ago. Her black coat with the fur trim sits well on her small frame, the brown short hair style fits her heart shape face well and her eyes look kind, the few lines around them are the only thing giving her age away.

She turns and makes her way towards Damien and me. Her arms are stretched out wide to pull him into her embrace; he never drops my hand holding me close.

"My boy" she says as she pulls him tight to her he towers above her, she is about the same size as Cami, he wraps one arm around her returning the embrace;

"Hello Mother" he says releasing her.

"Well, who is this beautiful young lady?" she asks Damien

"Mother, I would like you to meet Faith" he says and I force a smile. Why am I so disappointed that he never said girlfriend? I should be relieved knowing that he doesn't see me that way. It makes things easier right? But a small part of me wanted more, hell, who am I kidding, a big part of me wanted it.

She turns towards me and I feel Damien's hand release mine. I instantly miss the heat, putting my hand out to greet Lily, she quickly pushes it away and wraps me in a warm embrace. Momentarily stunned, I bring my arms up to return her hug. After a few seconds we pull apart.

"Hello Mrs. um…" shit realizing I don't even know their last name I look away embarrassed by my lack of information.

"Call me Lily dear." She says in the friendliest voice I have ever heard.

Anton is next to come and greet me, he just looks like a smaller less bulkier version of Malc except for his grey hair. He stands tall and you can see he has worked hard all his life, he is regarding me with the same amount of kindness that Lily did, I'm awed by such kindness.

"So Faith, it would seem we have much to discuss. Like how you have managed to hold my sons attention when no others have." I shrink away as she speaks not really wanting to go down this road and explain it all to with her.

"I don't know what you mean, I have not captured anything Lily." I say hoping to stop the conversation.

"Nonsense my dear, he is smitten, anyone can see it."

Before I can form a reply Damien cuts into the conversation.

"Mother, enough!" he scalds her

She stops her questioning but I can tell by the look in her eyes that she's not going to drop it. I guess I'm about to have a crash course in how to avoid his mother.

"Come on let's go and have some lunch." Damien suggests

We make our way into the kitchen to sit at the oak table and I see that all the place settings have been laid. I do love this room with its bi-folding doors that lead out to the garden at the back, so peaceful and tranquil.

As we all approach the table I feel his hand on my back guiding me to the seat beside him, this is twice now he has had me sit at his side. There he goes again. Doing things that give me hope that he wants more than just his body on mine and what a fine looking body it is. Shit I'm losing track again but just one thought about that body, it's enough to send me weak at the knees.

Pulling myself from my thoughts as we all take our seats, the staff place the meat cuts, salad and bread all down on the table for us to help ourselves. Conversation flows smoothly between everyone and I find my self-relaxing a little. I take a relaxing breath and fix myself a plate.

Lunch passes by without any issue, Lily and Anton are taken to their rooms, Damien, Malc and Jake all leave to go to do whatever it is they are doing which just leaves Cami and me.

We did have a great chat yesterday and it has eased the strain we were both feeling. The worry about what is going on has not eased but at least we know we are safe, protected between the three men, no one can hurt us.

“So, they seem really nice… Way nicer than I expected!” Cami says in disbelief.

“Why? Were you expecting something different?” I reply not wanting to cause another row between us.

“Don’t take it the wrong way Faith, I am not saying anything bad, they’re just… sweeter than I expected is all.” She says and I can see there’s no malice in her words.

“Sorry" I say, "you're the one who is always telling me not to judge a book by its cover.” I say to her.

I know that if I were to judge Damien from his appearance I would be running for the hills. His ruthless persona is just a front for his business. I understand that, I can rationalize it in my head. Work and home - there has to be a balance.

To think, if I had not seen the nicer side of him all those months ago, the caring, the protecting, I probably would have run out of that apartment and not even glanced back.

It was who he was when no one else was around that enchanted me, he made me feel safe.

“Faith!” I hear Cami shouting my name pulling me from my distracting thoughts.

“Shit sorry Cami I was miles away.” My every bloody thought is being consumed by him, I need to snap out of this shit, it's not going to work out, I chastise myself.

"So what do you fancy doing? There's the library or the sauna we can try if you want, we don't have costumes with us for a dip but we can just wrap a towel around us in the sauna." I ask, wanting to spend a little more time with her. I have missed her so much, so any way I can prolong the time that she is out of that room dwelling on her thoughts the better. It's what she did for me. I may not have left the house, but she always talked to me or we watched a movie, drank wine, she made me feel normal, that is exactly what she needs right now, she needs her friend.

"OH I fancy the sauna, you think it would be ok to go and use it?" she asks me with so much hope in her voice.

"I can't see it being a problem, Damien said to make ourselves at home, come on lets go." I grab hold of her hand pulling her up from the table heading towards the hall.

We go down the hall on the opposite side of the huge table in the middle, I have never been down this way before now, they must go through some flowers in this house every day they have had a new arrangement on top of that table, we are not talking small bunch from a petrol station, we are talking 'Flowers R Us' had a party in here. Don't get me wrong they're stunning, they just seem too extravagant.

We wander along the hall and that's when we see it, and the whole place just opens up. The Olympic size pool has loungers and a table around it, there is a Jacuzzi in the corner as you look along the wall. You can see the home gym through a glass wall. I think my mouth must be on the floor as I wander around the room, tucked away in the corner is the sauna door.

We spot the changing rooms for the pool and wonder in, quickly divesting ourselves of clothes we wrap towels around us from the heated towel rail.

Wow this place is amazing. It’s like visiting a luxury hotel with spa.

Opening the door the wooden room is at the perfect temperature, just waiting for us just to sit in and enjoy which is exactly what we intend to do.

“I could get used to this” I sigh when we have been sat in there a few minutes.

With my eyes closed and my body relaxing, I hear Cami’s quiet reply

“Me to” she whispers, and I know when we get through this there will be light at the end of the tunnel, for both of us life has a way of working that shit out.

Later on I am sat on the couch in the living room after not seeing Damien since lunch, it’s crazy how much I miss him being with me. How pathetic am I? It's been days since we were reunited, and whilst I have known him longer the feelings that have developed these past few days have really affirmed to me what I already knew. I'm totally in love with Damien…. Shit! I still don’t know his surname. I am going to put that at the top of my list of things to find out about him.

“Can we talk?” I look up and see Lily standing beside the couch, nodding at her she takes a seat beside me.

“I know you love him, he loves you too you know.” I’m shocked by her comment, she can’t be serious. Damien most definitely does not love me.

"Damien does not love me." I say a little too quickly. It's only after I realise I didn't deny how I feel, I guess there's no point.

"Look sweetie it's ok. I know, I can see it but I just want to make sure you are not deluded by all of this exterior and that you know who and what he is."

Her tone is soft but there is warning in it I'm not sure if she thinks I am a gold digger or just blind.

"Oh I know who he is." She looks shocked at my answer.

"Well, do tell me who you think Damien Volkov really is." Lily asks me.

So that's his last name, it is lovely how it just rolls off the tongue, it really does suit him, and before I get lost in my thoughts again I need to answer Lily.

Taking a big breath of air, well hear goes, she wants to know what I know, I will tell her.

"I have known Damien just over 6 months, at first I thought he saved me, but a few days ago I realised he wasn't the hero, he was the villain in this situation." I tell her hoping that it would be enough to get me off the hook.

"And what situation was that? Oh my dear, are you pregnant? Am I having a grandchild?" I laugh at her suggestion. I can see I'm going to have to spell it out. I really didn't want to, I knew about Bella and what she had been through and I really did not want to upset her.

"No! Jesus no. My dad owes Damien a lot of money, so I was taken. Apparently so that Damien could try and get him to pay his debt but he didn't want to pay, and said that Damien could keep me instead. I think his words were that I would be exceptional payment for his debt. Damien has told me, so please understand Lily that he did not want to keep me and no harm came to me from Damien." I shuddered when I spoke, thinking about Conner's hands on me again it was enough to bring a little bile back up into my throat.

"I can't believe, he would do anything like that, not after what we went through. Is that why you are here? Did he decide to keep you after all?" She's nearly in tears and I can't handle it, I have to fix this. I don't want her thinking badly of the only child she has left.

"No Lilly, I'm not here because of the debt, my father tried to take me, to sell me to someone else. In the process he hurt my best friend and Damien saved us both. He bought us here to keep us safe while they find him."

"Now that I do believe, but it does not excuse anything he has done up until this point. That boy and I will be having words. How could he be so stupid in the first place to even attempt to take you? Even if it was only to scare your father!"

I start to cry at her words and talking about it has dragged every emotion to the surface.

"I'm sorry to have caused your family more pain."

"Oh poor child it's not your fault, none of this is." She says whilst wrapping me in her arms and letting me sob against her chest.

I cry for everything that has happened to me, but most of all I cry for Bella, she never got to have her happy ever after. I am safe, I am wanted and I am loved, all the things that Bella should have had with her family.

"Come on now dear let's get a cup of tea, it makes everything seem better, well that's what my mother used to say."

I dry my eyes against the sleeve of my cardigan, and nod at her letting her know that a cup of tea is just what I need.

Sitting at the kitchen table with a cup of tea in my hand we are chatting about anything other than Damien, she talks about what it was like being the bosses wife and what was expected of her, but she said at the time she did not care because she loved him and would do anything for her husband, she told me how he became cold and hard as time went by and would do anything to get what he wanted.

I could sympathize with her, my own father was becoming the same except it was not power that motivated him, it was greed.

I look up to see Damien standing in the door way listening to us chat and I can't help the smile that touches my lips at the sight of him. Lily notices my smile and looks up to where he is stood and her face suddenly changes from soft to hard, calm to rage and I think if he was wearing red she would charge.

"You and I need to talk now!" she demands. Shit, this is not good his face falls and he looks at me one last time and nods to his mother and heads out of the room.

CHAPTER THIRTEEN

Damien

I FOLLOW MY mother into the office waiting for her to take a stand in front of my desk, it's usually where she takes her perch to scald me, arms crossed in front of her waiting, tapping her foot against the solid floor.

"Do you want to explain to me what the hell is going on Damien!" she exclaims

"Mother I'm not sure what you think you know or what has been said but I can explain." I let out a frustrated sigh. Since when do I have to justify myself to anybody, I am 30 years old for Christ sake, I run this family nobody else but me.

"You really need to explain to me, because I have just had to listen to that sweet girl in there tell me what she has been through and it broke my heart"

My mother's voice was cracking with emotion.

"Right, fine, you want to know what I did. I will tell you then." I growl, really not looking forward to hurting my mother any more than I already have. She has forgiven me for killing her husband. Even after what he had done she still loved him, she knew deep down that he was wrong to do it and she did leave him as soon as she found out, but giving up on everything you have and everything you have been for the last 20 years is not an easy fate.

Anton was a Godsend. He hated my father by this point, he helped pick my mother up and slowly piece her back together. How could a father do that to a child that he created, loved and cherished above everything else in the world, is just incomprehensible to me.

"I did take her mum." I admit to her my voice is sharper than I mean it to be.

"How could you? What were you thinking?" she scolds me, that look of pure disappointment and utter disbelief is etched on her face.

"I wasn't thinking. That's just it. I had a man who owed me £350,000, and he was avoiding me. So I told Malc to grab her, we were only holding her, making him want to pay up to get her back." I don't recognize my own voice.

"So, you became your father." My stomach turns at her suggestion. I am nothing like my father I would do anything to save Faith from any of this, I would never harm a hair on her head.

"I am nothing like him, I will never be like him!" I see my mother inwardly shrink at my tone. But she soon comes back to herself.

"Well tell me how this is different then? Because I fail to see it."

“When I saw her in that room, once she had woken up, she was cowering in the corner it brought it all back mum, then he said we could keep her and it killed me. It was like history repeating its self and I needed to break the cycle so I said I would get her out. And I did that, I got her out but what I didn’t expect was that I would have feelings for her. I became obsessed with her safety, I watched her, every single day, to make sure she didn’t come to any more harm.”

“So you are telling me you did all this because you like her? Can you not see that she has spent the last 6 months as a shell of the person she was before, and that my dear boy is not a woman you want to coddle because in the end you will make her hate you.” My Mother’s words are harsh, but true.

“I know Mother, I know, but her father comes back into her life and things have gone from bad to worse. We had Jake watching them, but her dad still managed to get into the apartment and he hurt her best friend so I brought them here to keep them safe, well mainly Faith.”

“So is her father that big of a threat to her?” she asks me, I can see that she likes Faith, it’s the only reason that she is taking such an interest.

“From what we know at this point he is hiding in plain sight. He has guards protecting him, that’s all we seem to be able to establish at this moment in time.”

I don’t want to tell her everything, she will only worry. Telling her we were going in to end him some time soon, would not be a wise decision. No my Mother needs minimal information.

“Look Mum, I know you don’t really understand and I am sorry but I can’t change how I feel when I am with her.”

"You don't think I understand what love is? Of course I do you silly boy! I watched the man I love sell my child, only to then have my other child kill him to avenge his sister. It ripped my heart out when the man he turned into was dead and cold and not the man I fell in love with. It's the man he used to be that I mourn and love with all of my heart, so don't try to tell me Damien, that I don't understand." I see the tears filling up in her eyes and they are threatening to fall down her cheeks.

"I'm sorry that all this has brought up old memories Mum and that you have been pulled into this, but I won't let her go, I can't." My words are full of pain I hate that I have caused it all.

"I know love. Of course you can't. You love her!" her words send me into a panic, I don't love her, it's not possible.

"I think you're jumping the gun a bit Mum. I like her and I care about her wellbeing but that's not love." I can't think along those lines, it will complicate everything and that is something that we don't need. Oh who am I kidding… it's already complicated.

"Ha! If you say so. No I'm not saying I agree with what you have done or can even begin to contemplate why you did it, but you are my son and I love you, so you will hear no more of this from me, I have said my piece. But don't try to pull the wool over my eyes. I know my son." She walks over to me and places a kiss on my cheek before heading out of the office.

I make my way over to my desk reflecting on what has transpired over the past few months. Is my need for power and revenge really turning me into him?

I pour myself a huge tumbler of whiskey, and swallow it in one go. Do I love her?

No, I don't. Am I infatuated by her body? Yes.
Speaking of infatuation I need her. Now!

Making my way to my room, I have a plan in mind and I want to follow it through.

She is sat on my bed with a book in her hand reading, when I walk in she looks amazing. The wave of lust hits me straight in the groin. She belongs there in my bed, in my home. She belongs with me and seeing her there intensifies my lust tenfold.

"Hey Damien, I'm sorry I told your Mum. She kind of cornered me, you're not mad at me are you?" her voice is sweeter than sin and my cock is straining against my slacks, I decide to play this out a little to see how far she will go.

"I might be mad at you." I say trying to mask the desire in my voice.

"Well I said I was sorry. What more can I do to make it up to you?" I can sense the smile there and I won't say it's not turning me on more because it is.

"You can start by crawling over here and showing me what else that mouth of yours can do." As I finish my words she places her book down on the bedside table and crawls across the bed towards me. The sight of her on her hands and knees is fucking sexy as hell. Her pace is slow and measured teasing me as she goes, her eyes sparkle as they lock onto mine, She comes to a halt inches from my crotch.

"What would you like me to do now?" she asks her voice is breathless.

"I want you to show me how sorry you are." I tell her, hoping she rises to the challenge. She sits back on her heels and her hands tentatively reach up to my zip, I feel the tug as she slides it lower and I clench waiting for the pop of the button.

“Is this what you want?” She says to me, and my God if it doesn’t make me harder hearing her voice like that.

“No what I want is your pretty mouth wrapped around my cock.” I put as much command as I can into my lust filled voice. It must work because she pops the button and starts to tug my pants down, when I feel the cool air hit my tip, I shudder wondering what she will do next. I throw my head back and close my eyes waiting for the sensual assault.

I wait and wait and it does not happen I look down to see her just staring at me stifling a giggle.

“What’s the hold up Faith?” I ask harshly wondering what’s so funny it’s not every day your waiting for a blow job that never happens; then they have to refrain from giggling, it could really wound a man's ego.

“Well I hope I’m getting something out of this?” the cheeky little minx turning the tables on me making me sweat like that.

“And what is it you want?” I question her.

“Well, I’ve heard that there is a position we can do where we both pleasure each other, that’s what I would like to try,” well fuck me sideways she wants to try a sixty nine? Bring it on baby. I can get on board with tasting her sweet little pussy.

“Get naked baby. Now. I want to see all of you before I taste you.” She gets up and strips down quickly, I almost shoot my load just watching her. I don’t want to wait another second. I get my shirt and trousers off throwing them to the floor as I lie on the bed and pull her down to me. When I start kissing her she opens up to me instantly. I want to feel all of her as

I glide my hands up and down her body tracing every curve, engraving it on my memory.

I pull away from her lips, and start kissing her neck when I get to her ear I whisper to her softly.

"I need you to turn around now baby I want to taste." She nods and turns around, her mouth now millimetres away from my cock. Her wetness is obvious right here at my lips and I can't resist. I dart my tongue out and lick from the top to the bottom. The quick jolt of her hips and the moan from her lips is all that I need to know that she is enjoying it.

I feel her mouth wrap around the head of my cock, and the warm cavern of her mouth is heavenly, I push my tongue inside her in slow jabs in and out, I hear her moans against my cock her head is bobbing up and down now, taking more of me deeper inside her mouth as she finds her rhythm, it is taking all of my restraint not to finish right this instant, but I need to bring her to her release first before I find mine.

As my tongue laps at her I thrust a finger deep inside her and start to pump in and out. I keep my rhythm steady, I concentrate my tongue on her clit. I can feel her getting closer so I keep going. I add another finger and thrust all the way inside and curl my fingers and it is enough, I feel her clamp around my fingers as she screams out my name with my cock still in her mouth and I can't hold on anymore. I release myself into her waiting mouth, hoping that she swallows it all down.

She turns and collapses at the side of me on the bed. I wrap my arms around her pulling her into me. This is where I want to be. Lost in Faith.

I don't remember falling asleep or if we even spoke to each other before we did. The next thing I know is the knock on my door and Malc's voice coming from the other side.

Stretching in the bed I look down to see that Faith is still fast asleep. I get out of bed as quietly as I can, pulling on my clothes from earlier. Taking one last look at the angel that sleeps in my bed. I head out of the bedroom.

I walk into the kitchen to grab myself a coffee, before I find out what Malc wants me for. I am sat at the table with my coffee in hand when Malc walks in and takes a seat at the side of me.

"Ah there you are, I have been looking for you. We need to discuss what we are going to do as we don't have a lot of time to pull this off, so we need to get our heads together."

"I agree but you need to remember this is not your personal mission Malc." He nods in understanding realizing that he is letting his emotions get the better of him.

We make our way to the office, Malc rang Jake in the kitchen and told him to get back to the house, I may not have liked how Malc demanded to get a plan in motion but he is right it needs to be done. I want my girl safe, and then we can concentrate on us.

Sat in my office there is Jake, Anton, Malc and myself. We are going over what little intelligence we have on Darren trying to see when would be best to take him out.

Jake has definitely done his research while he has been sat outside there every day. He has the number of guards that watch him, he also has the times they change shift, but above all, he has figured out his schedule. Where, when, who with and how many guards go with him.

I decide that it will be better to get him when he takes a trip out. Now to figure out when will be best.

My mind keeps wondering back to Faith lying in my bed. I can't wait to get this problem dealt with so that I can spend my time with her.

"So we have a destination." Jakes voice permeates the fog that is my brain at the moment.

"You will have to repeat the destination for me, I didn't catch it." I say with utter authority in my voice.

"We will grab him when he makes his trip to the massage parlour next. He seems to be the least guarded there so it makes sense" Malc states.

"Yeah that sounds like the best option." It seems that I am not with it at this moment in time and I only want to be with one person right now and I can't seem to focus on anything else.

"Right gents I am not really in this meeting right now and have other things that need attending to, we'll meet back in this room 9am tomorrow." The nods around the room let me know that they're on board and we all start to file out of the office. I know exactly where I am going.

Chapter Fourteen

Damien

"Come for me Faith," with my words she explodes around me as I thrust again, pushing myself over the edge to join her, feeling my release hit her, deeper than I have ever felt before.

Looking at her takes my breath away and I can't believe how lucky I am to have her here in my arms. I don't ever want to wake up and find her not there it would destroy me.

After coming back down I roll off of her and lie on my side looking at how beautiful she is. I see all of the beauty on the outside, but what astounds me is the beauty she has inside matches it perfectly. Just being with her makes me want to be a better man. For her. For me. She deserves the best, and I want to be that for her.

“Do you think what we are doing is wrong?” her question startles me and I’m not sure I like her train of thought. Why would she even ask that? Can’t she see how good we are together, how she was made for me. It’s right then, in that moment that I realise I can’t function without her.

“What do you mean Faith?” I ask, there is no way that I’m putting anything into her head. What she feels, what she thinks. It needs to be all her.

“You and me. How do we explain to people how we met? I mean, ‘oh you know, the normal way. He kidnapped me and we just kind of happened.’ It’s not normal Damien. People are going to think I have Stockholm syndrome or something. They're going to think you need to be locked up. I mean, I know we’ve not defined anything, but I can’t help my crazy thoughts”

Hell. This is not what I wanted to be dealing with first thing today, especially when I have to be back in the office in 30 minutes to sort out the plan for Darren.

“Hey what’s brought this on, have I ever hurt you Faith? All I want, all I’ve ever wanted since you woke up in that room is to keep you safe.” I ignore the defining us comment. It’s too soon to tell her that I think I love her, I don’t want to scare her away again. Plus as the days go on, that ‘I think’ is turning into an ‘I know’. I start to realise that it’s true, I’m hopelessly in love with her.

“No you haven’t hurt me Damien, but that’s not to say I have not been hurt because of you.” Her honesty cripples me. If I could bring Connor back and punish him again every day for what he did to her I would, but she’s right. She was hurt because of me, and I’m going to make damn sure it doesn’t happen again.

"I know Faith, and I'm sorrier than you'll ever know. I am doing everything in my power to keep you safe from Darren. I won't let anything else happen to you, but I need you here to do that Faith. Just give me some more time."

I was furious with myself for dragging her into this. Yes it may have started off wrong but it soon changed for me. All I wanted to do was keep her safe. She has to know that all I want to do is protect her. I have to keep the women, I have in my life safe, that's why my mother is out of London completely and she has Anton with her. I failed Bella, I won't fail to protect anyone else I love, that's what's driving me right now. The need to protect burns me up from the inside, it consumes me until I can't see anything but destroying the danger to those I love.

"No that's not what I am saying Damien. You're taking this all wrong. I meant us fucking because I know that that's all this is. Sex. Nothing more." How wrong could she is. She doesn't have a clue how deeply I care for her, though I suppose that's my fault too.

"You think this is just sex Faith? That this, what we have is just us fucking? Are you crazy? Blind? Or do you just not want to admit it? I have wanted you since you opened your eyes to me. I crave you Faith. I fucking *need* you. I know I stayed away, I thought I was best staying in the shadows, protecting you, without you knowing. Then the threat came back, and I knew then that I wouldn't be able to stay away any. I don't care what you tell people how we met, just as long as you say your mine I don't care." Her eyes softened in that moment and I knew the fight had gone from her, but I had to get through to her. She had to know how much she meant me. She's the only one with the power to break me.

"I need you Faith. You are the light to my dark, good to my evil. I'm so fucking in love with you it hurts. I've fallen so hard, loving you makes me want to be the man you deserve, but before I can be that for you, I have to destroy the danger surrounding you. What happens over the next few days Faith, it's going to be rough and I need to know that you're with me. I need to focus and I can't do that if I'm worried about you leaving." I let it all out. Everything. I've never done that, and as I look into her eyes I feel empty. All I can do now is hope that she saw the truth in my words.

"I love you Damien. I've loved you for so long but that's what scares me. Loving you doesn't seem right. I feel guilty for loving you, but whenever I think about you or feel you. It just feels right, I am with you. I'll be by your side throughout it all Damien. I'm yours."

She loves me? I don't know what I did to deserve her but I swear to God I'm not letting go. This might just be the best moment of my life. She fucking loves me. I roll back on top of her and bring my mouth down hard against hers, tasting her, savouring her, showing her what it will be like forever with me, because I will never have enough of her.

***

I see everyone waiting in the office when I arrive, I have a huge smile plastered on my face and Malc just raises an eyebrow at me.

I don't give at rats arse what these lot think, once today is over I will be able to see the light at the end of this long tunnel we have been in. I want the end because I want the life that I will have with Faith.

Getting to take her out, having her on my arm showing the world that she is mine and only mine.

"Good morning gents lets' get to work shall we." I see the guys all nodding and it pleases me having them on my side knowing that they will do what's necessary.

"So we have a place where we are going to get him, now we just need the plan of when and how?" I could not wait to get my hands on the slimy bastard knowing what he wanted to do with her again; selling her off for his own gain. It made me sick.

"I think we need to be inside waiting for him to enter the room and take him that way." Malc said but before I had time to respond telling him it was not a bad plan Jake piped up.

"No we need to grab him on the way to the parlour. That way we can take out the guards. We don't want them following us." His point was valid and I get to decide which was best. Oh goody!

I don't want anyone to follow but I want as little blood shed as possible. I don't really want to take the guards out. They're just paid to do what they have to. They have no loyalty to him.

The only person that needs to die is Darren and it will be by my hand.

"Both plans would work, but I think we need to do it at the parlour. Knock the guards out and then take him to the warehouse, by the time they wake up, we'll be long gone and his phone will be disabled so they won't be able to track him. I want as little blood shed as possible. I want this to happen in 3 days. Anton you need to go and scope the place out and report back with entrance and exit plans, they don't know you so they won't be looking for you, Malc you need to sort vehicles and weapons out, Jake I need you to get the warehouse ready."

I do love the power that comes with my position. The hold I have over these men knowing that they follow my command, the loyalty that comes with that. The power is heady but it's not everything. That's the one thing that separates me from my father. I have the respect of my men, not their fear.

"Do you think that's enough time to get everything set up?" Jake asks. How fucking dare he question me. He needs to learn his place, and fucking quickly.

"Yes it's enough time! You're either going to do the work in the time you've got or I'll find somebody else that will," I tell him in no uncertain terms. I won't hesitate to replace him. I need trustworthy, loyal people to stand beside me.

"Sorry boss. I'll head out now, and set it up. No disrespect intended." I nod at his words but I can see they're empty.

"Right boys, go and what you need to do. Report back here at 3pm and we will finalise all the details." With my final words they all get up to leave.

I run the numbers for a couple of hours until it was time for lunch, which gave me an idea. I wonder if Faith would like to go for a walk around the grounds. Would she like that? I don't even know. I know how her body reacts to mine, and what causes her to burn for me, but I don't know who she is. I don't know her favourite colour, how she takes her coffee, how she likes her eggs. Does she even like eggs? I stat to doubt if I'm cut out to be the man she needs. Maybe our relationship just sex like she said. Maybe that's what she was really getting at this morning. The thought brings me down a little. Once this is over I intend to get to know her, maybe the walk around the grounds would be the ideal start.

I finish my plan, the staff was very accommodating, it's not every day I give them a request like this. I make my way to the living room where I know Faith will be, most probably with Cami and my Mother. I hear the giggling coming from the room even before I enter; it automatically puts a smile on my face.

"He did not do that!" I hear Faith question, then my stomach drops when I hear my Mothers' voice reply.

"Oh yes he did, he ran right out of the door, naked as the day he was born, refusing to be bathed." The giggling starts again. I run my hand down my face, how could she tell her that one. I can't stand and listen to this a moment longer, it's a train wreck waiting to happen. I walk into the room and lean against the door frame. They all turn to look at me, and once they register it's me they burst into hysterical laughter. Man! She's already told them, I think I am going to kill my mother. How could she tell them that story I was 7 years old for crying out loud! I can't be held responsible for my actions. I wanted to be back outside playing with all my friends, rather than having a bath I slipped out of the bathroom and ran back outside to get away and hide but little did I know that my friends would be waiting. Everyone laughed at me and I ended up punching Malc in the face, and well lets' just say he never laughed at me again.

I mask my annoyance at my mother, and turn directly to Faith. She's wearing a summer dress that ties around her neck and I get a vision of untying her dress and watching it pool at her feet. I wonder if she is naked under the dress I might just have to find out.

"Faith, can I have a word please?" I ask my voice a little harsher than I meant it to be but after what I walk in on can she really blame me.

"Oh, of course." She stands up and makes her way to follow me. Once we're out of the living room I clasp her hand in mine and lead her towards the kitchen.

"What's the matter Damien? Where are we going?" she questions me. I look over to her as we walk to the kitchen and she looks worried

"I want to show you something." I tell her, any traces of anger and embarrassment are gone from my voice.

"Of course, I thought you were angry at me for laughing when you walked in."

"I'm not mad, embarrassed maybe, but not mad. Even if I was it would be at my mother for sharing the most embarrassing story there is about me. I hate it." I tell her.

"I think it was cute. I could just picture you as a kid, doing normal fun silly stuff. It was nice."

Hang on a minute she thinks it was cute? I am most definitely not cute!

We walk into the kitchen and I open the doors that lead into the back garden and take a step outside. It has been a long time since I have taken the time to appreciate the tranquillity that is my garden. Pulling her with me I walk with her deeper into the garden. I want her to enjoy this, it's a first for me. I don't do romance I have needs that had to be met and I always found someone willing to meet them but when I met Faith that changed. In her I see my redemption and my future all rolling into, one stunning little package with the emerald green eyes.

"Why are we out here?" she asks seeming a little confused I want to keep it a secret but I don't want her to be scared.

“I want to show you something that I think you will enjoy as I told you before, we are more than just fantastic sex, Faith.” I try to calm her as I lead her over the grass towards the bottom of the garden I love this place. It’s secluded and peaceful. It’s my favourite part of the house. It was what made me fall in love with the house when I bought it.

We walk to the secret garden and I hear the running water as soon as I step through the stone archway. There is a rock wall with the water cascading over it with a large rock pool at the base. I have LED lights that change colour under the surface and the terrace has been transformed since I was last here. The patio with the table and chairs look clean and neat but what really captures my attention are the vines that have grown up the pergola with the fairy lights woven through the open roof making them look like stars twinkling, it makes me determined to bring her back here at night. I hear her gasp beside me

“Oh Damien this is beautiful. It’s like something out of a fairy tale” It fills me with pride knowing that she likes it so much. I feel such a sense of joy to see the light in her eyes and her big, beautiful smile. I watch her as she takes it all in, her eyes growing wider when she spots the decking under the pergola. The table is set for two and I walk her over, pulling out a chair for her. I wait for her to sit down so I can tuck her in and take my seat opposite her.

“Will you have a picnic with me Faith” I ask, her cheeks flush and her eyes sparkle when I speak.

“You did all of this just for me? I can’t believe you went to all this trouble! Of course I would love to enjoy a picnic with you.” A genuine smile adorns my face and I let out the breath I did not realise I was holding.

“Yes I did all of this for you Faith. There is not ‘just’. You’re worth everything. Every minute of my time, everything that I can give to you and do for you. You are everything.”

***

We spend ages in the garden just indulging in each other. God how long has it been since I just did that, and I don’t mind one little bit that I only kissed her. Every moment with her is treasured.

We’re not far from the house when I feel her hand grip mine a little tighter, looking at her I see her chewing her lip as if she wants to ask me something.

“What’s the matter baby?”

“I need some more clothes Damien I only packed a couple of things and there are certain things I need.” She blushes while she is speaking and it’s the sexiest thing I have ever seen.

“I’ll send someone out to get you some clothes.”

“You most certainly will not send someone out to pick up clothes, underwear and toiletries for me. I’m perfectly capable of shopping Damien. I was merely telling you that I want to go into London and do some damage to my credit cards. I think I deserve it.” She says with a no nonsense tone that grates on my nerves.

“It’s not safe Faith.” I tell her I will not be letting her go shopping at a time like this.

“We need to go. Don’t do this, have one of the boys come with us if you must, but I need clean clothes. I feel like a tramp.”

I can see I am not going to win this argument. “Fine, but you can it wait until tomorrow?” She squeals and kisses me on the cheek. I swear I’m turning soft around this woman.

I'm pretty sure Jake can manage to watch the girls while they go shopping.

Chapter Fifteen

Faith

WE'RE ABOUT TO leave the house and I am ecstatic. It has been days since we've seen the outside world and I can't wait to go and get clean clothes.

I can't believe he gave in. Cami and I had been discussing how to bring it up all day yesterday. In the end it was down to me, it was just finding the right time. After our talk in the morning I didn't see him then until midday when he took me on a walk of the garden. He almost killed me with romance. It was perfect. The food, the setting it was magical and I loved every minute of it.

I waited until we were walking back towards the house to ask him. I didn't want to spoil our picnic and luckily he relented but only after I said my piece.

I woke up this morning feeling refreshed. I can't

remember the last time I got excited about shopping. Since finding out about Damien I'm not as anxious about things. Don't get me wrong I'm still worried about going outside but that's the fear of my father finding me.

Whilst I will never forgive him for what he did, if my father hadn't shown up, I would not have got Damien back. It's funny how things work out.

I make my way out of the bedroom to meet Cami and head out. I want to show her that in spite of all that has happened I'm still me, and that I'm finally getting back to who I was before.

Cami looks beautiful of course, she always did, her hair was glossy and straight, the blue tips still look majestic and her clothes even though it was just jeans and a t-shirt she had her trademark heels on, that's what makes her Cami.

"Are you ready to leave?" she asks and I can see a little fear in her eyes. I forget that this is a major step for her too. This is the first time she will have been out since what my dad did to her, but I know she won't give up. I will make sure of it. She pulled me out of hell and I'll sure as hell do the same for her.

"Yeah, come on let's get out of here for a bit." Looking around I don't see anyone else.

"Who is taking us?" I asked her really hoping Damien had managed to take the time so he could escort us.

"Jake is taking us, Damien and Malc are busy with work or something." I sigh, a little disappointed that Damien won't be joining us. At least this gives me more girly time to spend with Cami.

We sit in the back of the black Range Rover as we head towards London from Surrey. I hope the drive passes quickly as I count up what I need to get. I want to get some new underwear and clean clothes.

Cami and I catch up in the back of the car and the drive passes soon enough. I take in our surroundings and notice that we're not in the center of London.

"Jake where are we going?" I ask him.

"I just have to pick something up so I thought I could do it before we got to the shops."

"Oh, okay then." I look up at Cami and she still seems to be smiling so I lean further back into the seat of the car and think nothing more of it.

Twenty minutes later we pull up to a warehouse, the car comes to a stop outside and Jake pulls his phone from his pocket.

"Send the guys out, our guests have arrived!" A shiver runs through me. What is he on about? He ends the call and throws the phone onto the other seat, quickly I make a grab for the handle of the door only to find that it has been locked. I start to panic as I see the fear all over Cami's face. I realise that I don't even have my phone, when we left with Damien he said they could be traced so they never came with us something I am deeply regretting right now.

"What's going on Jake?" I ask him hoping that this is just a mix up and that the doors are not locked to keep us in but to keep someone else out.

"Well, you see I have a surprise for you Faith. There's someone in that warehouse who wants to say hello to you." The malicious look that covers his face knocks the breath out of my body. Gone is the quiet nice guy. He's been replaced by pure evil. He presses a button and the doors unlock.

"Go on, run. I dare you. It will just make it that much sweeter when I catch you." I don't move, I'm frozen. Not again. How many more times do I have to go through this shit. I feel the door next to Cami open as she throws herself out of the car and runs. I scream at her to stop. She's only going to make it worse for herself. One thing I learnt the last time, try not to piss them off. They really don't like it.

I see the men running after her as I scream at her. I'm distracted as my door opens and a man the size of a mountain grabs my arm and drags me from the car.

"Hey!" I snap at him. "Did I refuse to come out of the car? No. So get your hands off me, I can walk my damn self." I feel his grip lessen, only slightly, but I'm grateful for that much. At least I can feel the blood flowing back down it.

"No can do." The thug says so I try to walk as best I can whilst being man-handled. I hear screams and when I look I see Cami being punched in the face. She goes limp and the other guy who has hold of her flings her across his shoulder carrying her back towards the warehouse.

"Hey arsehole! Was that really necessary, or did hitting a woman make you feel more like a man. Prick." I yell at him. I feel so fucking helpless, and so ridiculously responsible. I just know this is my fault.

Walking into the warehouse I notice that it's just a bleak, empty space. *What the fuck is this place?* I see the yellow tarpaulin on the floor and I cringe inwardly. Why the fuck am I here, and why is Jake helping them? He's supposed to work for Damien!

I'm pulled further into the room and then shoved forward. I fall onto my hands and knees on the tarpaulin, they sting as they make contact with the floor. I keep my head lowered not really wanting to see what is going on.

“I like you on your hands and knees Faith.” Oh god I feel sick. Jake’s words disgust me. Why would he say something like that? I don’t look up, not wanting to acknowledge what he said.

“Enough!” I hear the boom that is my father’s voice and I snap my head up, meeting his eyes.

“Hello Faith, Jake you don’t own her yet, once I have had the confirmation that my debt it cleared, *then* you *can* do whatever the hell you like with her. I don’t give a shit, but for now, she’s still mine.” His words are cold long gone is the man I called Dad. He really has become a monster.

“Oh you’ll get your confirmation when you make the call later on today.” I hate not knowing. I am still on my hands and knees staying quiet trying to make myself small.

“What do you want me to do with this one?” I hear another guard ask I turn my head and see a knocked out Cami over his shoulder.

“Put her in the room and someone take this one as well we have work to be getting on with” Jakes voice rings out loud and clear.

I’m dragged into a room with nothing but a tatty dirty rug on the floor. The door closes behind me and I hear the distinct sound of the lock. I rush over to Cami and I try to wake her. That was some punch to the face. Her eye is swelling and her nose is bleeding.

“Cami. Cami” I whisper as I gently shake her shoulder, she starts to stir.

“Faith?” I hear her whisper

“Ssh.. It’s ok I’m here.” I say as gently and quietly as I can, I don’t know why I am so calm, I feel sick to my stomach but I know I need to be the strong one. I need to get my shit together for her.

“What’s happening Faith? I’m scared.” It breaks my heart listening to her. If it wasn’t for me she wouldn’t be here.

“I’m so sorry Cami! My Father is here and from what I can gather Jake is helping him but I have no idea why.” I say to her I don’t want to tell her about what I heard him say to Jake.

“What’s going to happen to us?” I don’t want to lie to her, but I don’t want to scare her either, I need to be strong for my best friend. I hope Damien gets to us in time because that’s one thing I’m sure we don’t have much of.

“I don’t know Cami, I wish I did but I don’t” she curls into herself and starts to sob into her knees when I finish speaking, I feel the silent tears start to fall down my cheeks, they’re more for her at this point.

“Up, now!” I hear Jake shout and I’m startled awake, I must have dozed off. I look over to Cami who is still sleeping and I gently shake her awake.

“Come on we don’t have all day, some of us want to have some fun.” When we don’t immediately stand he sends two guards into the room to collect us from the floor.

“Get your dirty fucking hands off us!” I scream into the face off the guard who is trying to get hold of me. I start kicking my legs hitting anywhere I can on.

“You stupid bitch” he says when I connect with his knee. I feel his hand smack hard across my face, the next thing I feel is the pull of my hair, as he pulls me behind him out of the little room, my head burns, the concrete floor scrapes my knees as I try to claw at her hands in my hair.

I am thrown onto the tarp and Cami follows me. I get myself up on my knees and I can see that we’re surrounded.

We have been in this place for hours surely someone knows we are missing by now. What if Jake has phoned and told him I have run away? No, what they would gain from that. I try to get a grip on the thoughts running through my head. I refuse to let the panic take hold. They won't break me.

"I want to play a game Faith, and you're going to tell me everything I want to know or your little friend is going to learn what it is to be used in every way possible. Believe me, the boys are looking forward to ruining that pretty little thing. But, if you tell me everything I want to know I will let you go back to that room unharmed. For now at least."

Jakes voice is pure evil a far cry from what I have heard these past few days, I don't know what happened to make him this way.

"You sick twisted fuck! What is wrong with you?" Jake smirks as one of his men steps towards Cami and grabs her by her hair. There is no way I am not going to let them touch a hair on Cami's head, so I will have to play his sick and twisted game.

"Fine" I spit. I'll play along for now, hopefully he'll think I'm playing by his rules as I try to think of a way out of this.

"Good girl." I shudder at the tone of his voice, it makes my blood run cold. "Let's start shall we. I want to know everything, do you understand?" I was quickly coming to hate the sound of his voice but I just nodded waiting for him to start with his questions.

"Let's start with the easy things first shall we." it was more of a statement than a question.

"Have you and Damien had sex?" I coughed at his question, what sort of fucking question was that. When

I hesitated with my reply he started to walk closer to Cami, she tried to back away from him but muscular arms gripped a hold of her and held her still.

"Yes!" I scream anything to get him away from Cami. I won't let him touch her. He stops his approach and turns to me.

"Well I must say I am disappointed that it took you as long as it did to answer. I thought you wanted to protect your friend. I even started out with a question I already know the answer to, so that I would know if you were lying."

The questions seem never ending, it seems like he wants to know everything about positions, length of time, whether he came inside of me what made me scream, then when he seems to have enough with me answering questions he pulled himself from his jeans and started to get himself off. Right in front of my face. I knew he was a sick fuck but this was something else, and when he came, he came on my cheek, making me vomit. I can hear Cami's cries behind me at what she's being made to watch. I want to curl up into a ball and cry. I have never been so humiliated and debased in all my life. I thought what I went through before, and compared to this, that's nothing.

He tucked himself away and knelt down so that he could look directly at me.

"The next time you see me cum it will be inside of you eradicating every trace of him from your body. I will fuck you on top of his cold dead body and there is nothing you can do about it. I will own you. In every fucking way."

His words made my heart sink. How could my dad sell me to anyone, especially this sick fuck. What hurts the most about is not the fact that he said he would own me or the fact that he was going to fuck me, it's the fact that he plans to hurt Damien. It's that that brings tears to my eyes.

"Take them back to the room. Darren has a phone call to make and we have a plan to put in motion, only then you will get your paperwork and be free to leave Darren."

We're dragged back along the corridor and thrown into the little room. They locked us in there again with nothing. No food or water. Nothing.

I wipe my face as best I can with my top, trying my hardest to get rid of all traces of him, Cami is rocking in the corner. Once we were alone she lets it all out, they hit her a few times when she was screaming for Jake to stop what he was doing.

"I'm sorry Cami, this is all my fault. I'm so, so sorry!" I didn't hear a reply, she just continued to rock, her tears falling freely.

I understand now what Damien meant when he said, we need to eradicate the evil that's trying to destroy us. How can our love be wrong? Not once has he ever made me feel like I do now, he cares for me, even in the beginning he let me eat, drink and bathe. He gave me a bed to sleep on, not once did he hit me. He may be the head of the family, a ruthless killer, but that's not all he is.

I just need to figure out a way to keep Cami and myself safe until he gets here, because I have no doubt he is coming.

Damien will come, he always does when I need him.

Chapter Sixteen

Damien

"WHERE THE FUCK are they, damn it find them!" They left at nine this morning, it's now seven and they have not been heard from all day. If anything has happened to her I will lay waste to the world. I swear to any God that is listening, I will kill anyone that has harmed her. She is mine, and I protect what is mine.

I storm into my office, Anton is waiting for me. Good, I know what I need him to do, I just hope he can do it quickly.

"Can you trace a number for me? I need to know what has happened to the girls. They're with Jake." I say to him hoping that he will get on with it. I have never cared before how it's done, but now I can't help but want to know. I can't seem to get this feeling of dread out of my stomach.

"Of course give me the number and I will get on with it, do we have a name and address to go with it? It will make it much easier." I walk around to my desk and open the draws pulling out the information I hold on Jake Masters. It's not much but it's the basics he doesn't really have any background details.

"This is great I will get onto it now, give me an hour." I nod letting him know that's fine but on the inside it's tearing me up I want answers now not later.

The ringing phone pulls my attention, quickly answering it in the hopes it might be Jake or Faith, but it's Malc.

"What!" I bark at him, my patience is wearing thin and I want answers now.

"They've not been back to the apartment," he's as pissed off and worried as I am, he's just better at handling it than I am, well what the fuck has happened to them then?

"Fine hurry up back if there is no sign of them." I hang up wanting to keep the line clear for when Anton calls and I know he will call, within the hour he never leaves me waiting.

I'm sitting at my desk thinking about my girl, I'm really losing my shit about what could have happened to her. The phone rings it's Anton. *At last*.

"Anton." I say my voice is full of apprehension.

"I have the information you need, I am just letting you know that I will be with you soon." The edge in his voice has my anxiety reaching new level. What could be so bad that he couldn't tell me over the phone.

"Why can't you tell me over the phone Anton?" I question him. "Just trust me on this Damien, you do not want to hear this over the phone." He doesn't give me chance to reply before the line goes dead. What choice do I have but to wait.

The knock at the office door makes me jump a little, I see my mum looking red eyed and puffy, she's been crying. I can tell just by looking at her that she is worried about Faith and Cami but I'm guessing that all of this has brought back painful memories of Bella.

She walks in and I open my arms for her. I understand she needs to be held right now and who am to deny her what she needs. I think I need this as much as she does. I need someone to understand the pain I'm feeling. I'm not sure what has happened to them, but from what Anton said, it can't be good.

I wrap my mother in my arms and listen to her as she cries against my chest, we've not done this since Bella's funeral. After a few minutes she pulls out of my arms and reaches up to wipe the tear that has fallen down my cheek. She straightens up and asks the staff to put on a dinner even though it's so late. She knows as well as I do that until I have some answers, I won't rest, but I don't think my stomach will keep anything down.

I head to the gym while I am waiting. I don't even bother to get changed, I just take my shirt off and start at the punch bag. If I don't hit something, I will end up killing someone. Right now I want to feel the pain against my knuckles and the sweat running down my back. I let off steam for a good half hour, blow after blow I rain down but nothing seems to help ease the anxiety that I feel right now.

Back in the office after I quickly rub off the sweat and put my shirt back on, I sit myself back down at my desk, Malc is now sat in front of me, his toe is tapping on the floor and it's driving me mad.

He is worried about Cami, I can see it written all over his face He wants to break something just like I do.

"I can't get rid of this feeling that something is wrong," he says to me, and it's a tone I am not used to hearing from Malc, it's desperate. What can I say to him? I can't even reassure myself. Today is shaping up to be one of the worst days I have ever had. I have felt loss and pain, but nothing compares to the thought of losing Faith.

"We'll do everything we can to find them friend." There is nothing else I can say, so why bother trying to give the situation false hope.

"I know but that does not make the worry any better." With every word he speaks I feel his pain.

"I know my friend, I am the same. I don't even know what has happened to *moya lyubov*." The Russian flows off my tongue with ease at the moment, I know right then that the words are true.

"I've been waiting for you to realise that brother. I just wish it wasn't the worry that made you realise. I have not heard you speak our mother tongue for a long time my friend."

"It's only since Faith has been around, it fits, and it feels right."

"Well it's great to hear you speaking it again."

My mobile phone rings in my pocket and I quickly pull it out to answer.

"Yes" I bark down the phone.

"Hello Damien, something tells me you are couple of guests short this evening." Bile rises in my throat when I realise who it is on the phone and my worst fears are confirmed. Darren Young is on the other end of this line and it's then that I realise he has my girl.

"What do you want Darren? If you have laid one finger on them your dead," I see Malc visibly pale in front of me before his anger rises to the surface.

"That's not any way to speak to the man who controls what happens next, do you understand Damien? If you want to see these girls back alive and in one piece you are going to do exactly what I say."

"How do I know that she is still alive Darren? I am not going to play ball without knowing if she is still alive."

"You want proof of life, is that it Damien?" I hear him shout to someone to go and get Faith, and my hearts sores at the thought of speaking to my girl. Fuck, he really has her and with that my heart sinks all over again. I will kill this motherfucker if it's the last thing I do.

"Speak you worthless bitch," I growl at how he speaks to her.

"Hello" I hear her voice, it sounds so hopeless. I let out a breath and try to find my voice so I can reply to my girl.

"Baby are you ok?" I need to hear her voice.

"Damien, oh god please Damien get us out of here! My dad and" but before she finishes what she was going to say, I hear Darren's voice telling them to get her back into the room. I can hear Faith screaming, as she's pulled away from the phone. I swear to god when I find her I am going to fucking kill them all.

"So you have your proof of life, now I will tell you what is going to happen, you're going to nod and smile and do as you're told, if you ever want to see her again." I do my best to keep a lid on my temper but I can feel it starting to rise.

"Tell me what you want then Darren." I spit out

"Well for starters, I want £100,000 and my debt wiped. You're going to personally deliver it to me, and then when you do you can take the girls unharmed and we can go our separate ways."

"When and where do you want this to happen?" I grab a pen and paper off the desk and prepare to write down what he tells me. The fact that he has managed to get hold of her is pissing me off. Yet again Jake has fucked up, why the fuck would I let him watch her I should have learnt my lesson the first time. I have no-one to blame but myself.

"You will meet me tomorrow at 12 pm at your warehouse and I want you on your own. If I see anyone else I will kill them both do you understand?" I clench my fists tight by my side

"Fine!" before I can say anything else the line goes dead. I can't believe that fucker chose my warehouse, why the fuck would he think that it's ok to hold them at my fucking warehouse. I am going to put a bullet in the fucker.

"What are we going to do?" Malc says to me his voice is still thick with emotion.

"We're going to do whatever he says for now, we don't have a clue how many people he has working with him." I say to him, hearing groans as his reply so I continue. "We haven't got a clue how they managed to get the girls or if he has Jake as well." This whole thing is a mess but what else can I do. I just hope my words are enough to placate him, as once Malc gets hold of something he's all guns blazing, and that's not what's needed right now. We have to play it safe. This is more than just money, it's my girl on the line, and I need her more than anything in this whole damn world.

"I hope you know what you're doing Damien, because it's not just you with something to lose this time."

It's then that I realise my friend's feelings are just as much at stake as my own.

We sit for a while going over the plans of the warehouse looking at the surrounding area to see where the best point for Malc and Anton to stay out of sight. Anton may be old but he is far from past it, he guards my mother, he has done more than I will ever do in the time that he has been with my family.

There is a knock at my office door and I shout for them to come in, not wanting to peel my eyes away from the research I am doing on my own fucking property.

"Damien you might want to listen to what I have to say," Anton says I can tell by his tone this is serious. I look up from the blue prints from the warehouse to see him with a murderous look on his face.

"What is it Anton? What was so important that you could not tell me over the phone?" He walks over and sits down at the desk and I wait for him to begin telling me what's going on.

"How well do you know Jake Masters?" as soon as he says it, I know that my initial feeling about him was right.

"All I know is that he met Malc in a café, and Malc brought him back here to work with us, he's been with us a few months, the background check we did on him didn't turn up anything suspicious."

"Well I tried to traced his phone and came up with nothing as it was switched off, so I changed tactic and checked out his known address, there was nothing of note at first, it just looked like a rundown apartment with second hand basic furniture inside. When I went into his bedroom, that's when things got interesting." This is why I keep Anton around as he has a skill that you can't find in many people. He is ruthless, every task he takes on he is meticulous. He checks his information and then checks it again like he says "in life or death there is no room for error or bad judgment".

"How did it get interesting? How does this relate to Faith?" I ask him.

"I want you to listen to me Damien, and hear me out until I have said every word." I sit up straighter in my seat and prepare myself for whatever it is he has to say to me. I already know that I am not going to like whatever it is he has to say.

I nod giving him my word that I won't interrupt him.

"I walked around his apartment and saw nothing much until I entered his bedroom, there on his nightstand was a picture just lying on the top. The picture was of Jake with Conner, so I made a call to try and get more info on him. Damien, Jake is Conner's brother."

"FUCK!" my loud curse stopped Anton and he just pinned me with a look that said shut up there is more, I nod for him to continue.

"As I was saying Damien that is not the only thing that I found. He had pictures. A LOT of pictures of Faith and you, some of just Faith, it seems that he has been watching her for months. This guy, let's just say he has a total hard on for Faith, some of those pictures… No-one but you and her should see that shit. From the looks of it, he has been, let's say, fantasizing about Faith."

The dirty motherfucker. When I get my hands on him I am going to kill him, just like I did his brother and I won't even blink. To think of him using pictures of Faith to get himself off makes me feel sick. She is fucking MINE!

"Do you have any idea what he is up to? Or where he is now?" I ask Anton, I can see Malc sat in the chair his hands are gripping the chair, his knuckles are white with the death hold he has. I know he will blame himself for this because he brought him into the family. He is not to blame, we did the checks and did not find anything to connect him to anyone dangerous to us.

When I think about it, he has been there when things went wrong or did not happen as I planned them.

"Yes I know where he is" he sighs.

"Where is he?"

"At the warehouse Damien." I see the look of shock on Malc's face and that's when I know I heard him correctly.

This motherfucker is going to die.

Time to hunt.

Chapter Seventeen

Damien

I HAVE GONE through this plan over and over again, and it still doesn't sit right with me. What I can't fathom is why he has planned whatever he is doing to such detail. He's had plenty of opportunity to take me out and that's what makes me think it is not just me he wants and I will kill him for even looking at her. I can't get over that we have had this going on under our noses and we didn't even have a fucking clue.

I sent Malc out about an hour ago, he is no use to me when he can't think straight. His rage was at boiling point after he heard what was going on, he threw my chair against the wall in his fit of rage. I need him to cool down and get his head in the game that means detaching himself from the situation, closing off his emotions.

Anton sits in the seat that is still available and I know he has more to say about the whole deal, but he is holding back and I want to know why. Even if he is my elder I am still the head of this family.

"What are you hiding my friend?" I ask him wanting to give him the chance to tell me before I lose it completely. My sense of calm went out of the window when I learned that scumbag had *moya lyubov*. I am trying to hold it together as best I can but as the hours pass by it gets harder. I need to get her back here safe with me. I don't know what has happened to her or if she is ok. God help anyone if they have hurt her. I swear right now that they won't ever wake up.

Once I get her out, and I will get her out mark my words, she will be back home where she belongs.

Is it wrong that this has made me realise now more than ever that I can't live without her? No that's not it, I just don't want to live without her. She belongs by my side and that's where she will be for the rest of her life she will be mine.

"There are things I found out that I will never be able to erase from my mind Damien, and it's not thoughts I want you having about Faith or it will make you irrational and unpredictable. That is not something you need right now." Anton says to me, his thick Russian accent is more noticeable when he is angry. What the fuck is he going on about? All of these secrets and lies. This bullshit really gets to me, when I ask a question I want an answer, not some cryptic clue. I just want everything laid out in front of me

"Just tell me everything Anton. I need to know what I am walking into tomorrow." I am a little more forceful this time making him realise it's an order not a request.

"You really want to know what I found?"

"For fuck sake, yes! Just spit it out already."

I understand what he is saying I really do, I just want to have all the information so I can make the right choice. I need to get her out of this nightmare.

The things Conner did to her, I wonder if Jake has told her who he really is, if he has, then she will be reliving the hell she went through with him.

"I saw the pictures and tokens that he has kept from each victim." My stomach drops.

"What are you talking about Anton? Just tell me what you know." he nods his head and continues.

"There were pictures of women after he had raped them, and slit their throats. In some of the pictures, it was Conner doing the raping and slicing at the same time. There must have been over twenty pictures. It seems that they got their kicks from doing this and now he has the two girls and a very deep hatred of you. You took away Conner from him. If you don't play this right it's not going to end well for any of us."

I despise rapists. Men who get their jollies off from overpowering women and then taking away their right to say no, they're not real men. That's why I did what I did to Conner, to make him pay for what he tried to do to Faith. The rot that was in him is in his brother, I will do exactly the same to him, I will cut off every appendage he has used and I will tell him right at the end when I finally give him that deadly blow that will let him meet his maker, I will tell him that I enjoyed killing his brother and that I will rest easy knowing women are safer with the two of them dead.

I feel sick, I cannot bear to think what might be happening to Faith. I only just got to her in time the last time. I don't know if I would cope if I did not reach her in time again. Knowing that what we have is so much more than what it was back then, it kills me to think of any part of him touching any part of her.

“What were the tokens that he kept?” I question Anton, needing to know all the details, not that I want all that swimming around in my head, but I think it’s the only way I can prepare for what’s to come.

“He kept a lock of hair and their underwear that obviously had not been washed.” What sort of sick fuck did this? My mind is reeling. I want to go and hunt him down right the fuck now and put a bullet in his skull.

Tomorrow has to go to plan. It failing is not an option. I won’t give up. I can’t.

“Right we need to get this plan locked down, I don’t want any details left out. He will not get away with this, I won’t let him Anton. I understand why you didn’t want to tell me but I needed to know how bad it was.”

After a time I leave the office and go in search of Malc. I have not seen him since I had sent him out of the office. And with what Anton told me I am glad he was not there. He would only blame himself more.

I find him in the gym punching the bag. I can see the sheen of sweat that coats his skin, his pained cry alerts me to his hands. When he would not give up hitting the bag it was then I saw that he was punching the bag bare.

No strapping on or any gloves, his knuckles where red raw and I needed to get him to stop.

“Malc Stop!” I yell at him but nothing was getting through his haze. I walked closer to him knowing that any wrong movement and he would swing for me, not seeing anything but his pain.

As I got closer I saw the anger all across his face, his fists continued to pound against the bag.

"I heard what Anton said! I heard every last word how could I have brought some sick fuck like that into the family Damien? How could I do it to the girls, put them at risk like that?" I hate the fact that my friend is broken like this, it was bad enough that I was feeling the same way but I had to keep that mask in place to keep up the facade that everything would be ok when all I was thinking on the inside that I was about to lose my heart.

"You weren't to know who or what he was all we can do now is to try and fix it. Wallowing like this is not going to bring them back. I need her back whole Malc. Do you get me? I need your head in the game, close off your emotions like I have had to." I can see the pain slowly fade from his eyes as he turns to me. I need to know he is with me, right now I need him not as my friend but as my second.

"I'm with you, we may need to go over the plan again I was zoned out a little before, too wrapped up in my own shit to help you with yours."

"Right, well we need to find Anton and get this shit finalized. It happens tomorrow."

He nods his agreement and we head out of the gym towards the kitchen, thinking that's where he would be. I can smell my mother's cooking and if she is cooking Anton will be close by. He always was, it's funny to think that if it was not for my dad all this could have played out so differently. He adores my mother, I do think he has loved her all these years but would not go against my father. I suppose they got closer when I took over and sent Anton with her to protect her, I knew he would protect her until his last breath.

Walking in I see my mother sat at the table with a coffee in her hand and a plate of scones with jam and cream. I do love my mother's scones they are heavenly, across from her I see Anton with a couple of scones on his plate tucking in like it was his last meal, which I suppose, if things go wrong it might be. With that thought I sit down at the table and I place a scone on the plate in front of me.

Malc sits with us, but just grabs himself a cup of coffee and sits brooding while he waited for us to get on with planning.

"Mother would you give us a few minutes please, there are things we need to discuss." I hated having to get my mum to leave, but we were all here and I did not want to waste further time by going to the office to make plans.

"Of course dear. Boys, if you will excuse me I am going to take my coffee in the living room." With that she made her way out, leaving us to discuss business. I wait a few moments for the staff to leave the room before I speak to them.

"I liked the idea you proposed before Anton, but it's not without its risks. I think I need to go in dark. We can't let him think we are onto him." I hear Malc grunt and then Anton chirp in.

"You can't do that, how will we know if you're ok? We have to make sure we know what's going on at all times, you are the head of this family and you're knowingly walking into a trap, you do realise that don't you?" I have listened to him groan on and on it was bugging me to no end now.

"Look I will do whatever it takes to make sure she is safe, I will lay down my life for hers if it means she walks free from all of this, You two just have to do what you are told to do. Am I clear?"

I hear Malc grunt his agreement but looking Anton

in the eyes I could see the defiance in them.

"Fine!" he spits out knowing that I needed his compliance.

"So you and Malc will hold back and stay hidden while I attempt to make the drop, then when I'm taken inside or whatever their plan is, you wait one hour. I need to establish if the girls are safe and ok first before you two come in."

I knew the plan was risky, to go in unarmed and without a way to communicate with my them, but we couldn't let him think we had the upper hand.

I would act surprised and do my best to play along but I won't be held accountable for my actions if I see a mark upon her body. I will make him pay for any pain he has caused, just like his brother did.

"So what do you want us to do? Kill and extract or capture and torture?" Malc asks. I let his question swim around for a minute. What do I want to do? I want to be the one to kill Jake, just like I did his brother.

"Kill everyone but Jake you save him for me. I want to make sure he gets it slow and painful just like Conner."

It is the first time in days I felt a little in control. I need that control, it is my anchor. The thought of losing Faith is killing me, but I will see her back with me.

"Yes boss."

We spend the next hour hashing out all of the little details and scenarios for if and what might happen. We calculate what weapons and man power will be necessary to get the job. Anton is sorting the men we need, he says he can get men that will follow orders with no questions asked and right now that's what I need. The cars are all loaded up, ready and waiting to go at first light.

I went to the bedroom, the one we've shared and it feels empty. I can't bear the thought of going to bed without her. I can't face waking up in the morning without her in my arms.

So I must embrace the darkness once again to find my light and bring her home.

Chapter Eighteen

Jake

I AM SAT in the office of the warehouse, thinking about the last couple of days and how this plan of mine is coming together. I can almost taste the sweet fucking revenge I am going to have. Not long now until I can do what I want to her.

Revenge is what is driving me. It fuels my every waking action, motivates me to see this through. He killed my brother because of this fucking whore.

I need to feed the demon inside of me. I crave the darkness that is consuming me, and I drift closer to it every day.

I want to see the life drain from his eyes, as I do to him exactly what he did to Conner, I will see this through, I will have my revenge.

Darren Young has been a great tool, he has done what I have asked of him. He hasn't long got off the phone with Damien, and I so wanted to go up to him and snatch the phone away and scream at him, that it was me controlling everything. That it was me that took the girls, I wonder how he is feeling right about now after that call. Knowing full well her dad has hold of them. I bet Damien was climbing the walls trying to figure it out, so that he can get them back. There will be no coming back from this. But his usefulness has come to an end. If he thinks he's going to get that paperwork then he has another thing coming. He will never see outside of this building.

I think about the way I can do this, I want to see Faith's eyes when I kill her father in front of her. I am thinking of doing it today because I have to prepare for Damien tomorrow. That is the kill I am going to get most enjoyment from. Seeing the torment in his eyes as he watches while I take her, to watch as he dies inside knowing that she will never be the same .

I need to get this prick dealt with, and the sooner the better, I want to concentrate on the main event. I call Darren into the office. I want to make this quick, but I also want to torment Faith while I do it, and let her know that I mean business. What I do to her father is going to be like a walk in the park compared to what I am going to do to her and that fucker Damien.

"I want the girls brought from the room" I tell him, his look tells me that he does not understand why I want them.

"Why, what do you need to do that involves them? I made the call and you have them here." This little prick is really starting to piss me off. I should just shoot him right here where he stands and be done with it. Where would the fun be in that though, I want to toy with my prey a little before I complete the kill.

"You want that paperwork? You get the girls in that room along with yourself in 30 minutes, am I clear?" I tell him trying my best to keep a lid on my temper. It would be so easy to blow right now, I just want him out of the way, and the sooner the better really. He just nods and leaves. I love the power you can hold over people when you have something they want, people will do just about anything.

I try to calm myself thinking about all the other girls I have had. The thought of killing the girls is keeping me hard, and I haven't done one since before Conner died. This will be my first one on my own and I can't wait. It's been too long since I have fed my beast. My craving kicks up a gear at this rate I won't be able to control myself until tomorrow. I know after the kill I will need to satisfy the need within, but I can't touch Faith until I have Damien at his weakest, strung up and helpless. I suppose I could go to a bar and pick up some random slut to fuck tonight just to take the edge off, but I can't risk anything going wrong tomorrow, it all needs to go perfectly. Then it hits me, what I will do. A small smile plays across my face at the thought.

***

Thirty minutes later I see the girls knelt on the tarpaulin, and fuck if it does not start to make me hard. Seeing their heads down looking at the floor the tears probably sliding down their cheeks. I see Darren stood off to the side, there are two guards over by the doors and two guards behind Faith and Camilla. I checked before I left the office that my gun was fully loaded hidden in the waistband of my trousers at the back, hidden from view by the suit jacket that I have on.

I know the guards won't bat an eyelid when I tell them act. I walk closer to the girls. My steps precise and methodical. I have planned what I want to say, I want to put the fear of God into her for tomorrow. So far, she has not shown much fear when I have spoken to her. Anger yes but not fear. That is something I need from her and I know just the thing to do to do it

My plan is pretty simple. Kill Darren while Faith watches on her knees. This evening's entertainment is going to be so much fun.

"Darren can you come to stand at my side while I address the girls" I ask in my most sincere voice, it must be right as he does not even question me, he just moves to my side.

"Now then girls I want to tell you a little story, one of which you will not have heard before." I say to both of them as I speak, Faith's head snaps up in my direction and I can see the fire in her eyes, her spirit is still not broken. But that is something I am about to change with these words. They should have her reeling back into the shell of a person she was before Damien made himself known to her. I can't wait to be the one to burst her bubble and add to the shit storm that is her life. Not that she will have a life much longer if all my plans work out the way I want them to.

Camilla keeps her head down staring at the floor I can tell all this has already broken her, it was easy with her she has no fight in her not like Faith. The guard outside the room they are in said he heard her cries all night.

"Do you know who I am, Faith?" I question her, I can see that she is thinking about what I have said.

“Yes you're Jake and you work for Damien.” She answers me not a hint of fear in her voice, she is not quiet when she speaks. She looks me straight in the eye as she delivers her answer. I do admire that trait but that is what I am going to have the most fun breaking.

“You’re only half right there, see I have known about you for over 6 months” I see confusion play across her face but she does not lose eye contact, she keeps her stare focused upon me and me alone.

“I am sure you would have known about me, as you have been working for Damien, he said he had been keeping me safe since he left me at the hospital.” She replies. I don’t think I will tell her just yet. I will wait until I have killed her father who is still stood at the side of me the prick, has not said a word.

“We are getting slightly off track now. I am going to tell you how I came to be working with him.” I say pointing at Darren to my side.

“You see the day you went out with Camilla, I was on duty to watch over you and I did, but I saw it was your father who came and I delayed calling, I wanted to see what would happen but they still managed to show up just in time. And I let him give me a couple of punches to reprimand me so to speak.” I can see her trying to connect the dots and she won’t get it without all the pieces of the puzzle.

“So you’re playing both sides. Don't you think that Damien will figure it out and know what you are up to?” I cut her off when my hand meets her cheek not wanting to hear any more. The sound the slap bounces off the walls, her audible hitch of breath is the only clue that she gives, to let me know that she felt it, no cry of pain, nothing. For a woman she is holding up well better than most.

I can understand now why Conner was so infatuated by her. She's beautiful and has a very smart mouth but that's the appeal. You can see the strength she is finding deep down inside of her. She is trying to fight her fate with everything she has.

"No and he still does not have a clue so when he walks in here tomorrow and I get the pleasure of killing him, I will take great joy in telling him he had a traitor amongst his men."

Her head drops a fraction when I mention killing him, and it's the first time I see her have a slight defeated look on her face, even if it's only for a brief moment.

"I won't let you kill him" she whispers, it was so quiet I almost missed her saying it.

"You don't have a fucking choice!" I shout at her. The look in her eyes when I raise my voice is one of anger and pure hatred.

"Now back to what I was saying, you have a choice to make, how do you want me to kill your father? Would you like him to be shot in the head or shot in the chest either way he is getting shot, the choice is yours Faith." I hear Darren gasp at the side of me as if he has just heard what has been said.

"You can't do this!" He pleads with me "We had a deal!" When I don't answer straightaway he tries to move from my side, I nod to the guards by the door and they make a move to grab him.

"I think you will find I can do whatever the hell I want Darren, I have no use for you, you're expendable." When I see they have him held tightly so he won't be moving I look back at Faith who has a slight smile playing across her face. What the fuck why would she be smiling at the choice I asked her to make it's almost as if she does not mind him being shot.

"I need your choice Faith, what is it going to be?" This isn't as much fun as I thought I would. My thinking is that she should be crying and pleading with me to spare him, not shoot him. But nothing like that leaves Faith's lips.

She has them turned up and pressed together in what I could only say is a devious smirk.

"I would say shoot him in the heart but he does not have one, so shoot him in the head. I don't give a shit what happens to him after what he did to me, so do whatever you want to him."

I see it's not just me that finds him expendable in that moment. This is definitely not what I expected to happen, maybe I did underestimate the hatred she feels for him after what he has done to her.

"Please Faith, I'm sorry don't let him do this to me, I'm so sorry princess. I love you." Darren pleads with Faith and I don't know if his little statement will have any effect on her.

"Ha don't make me laugh. You don't know what love is, if you did you would never even have considered telling Damien to keep me, and then when that did not work you try to hurt my friend when I won't go with you, then to top it off you work with this scumbag." She screams every word at him while looking directly in his eyes. She is not backing down.

"Right, I think we have established that she wants you shot in the head and not the heart. So let's crack on shall we."

He fights the guards that hold onto him.

"You were supposed to protect me, not hurt me how can you hold me like this! Let me go." He is still trying to get his words out even when it's pointless. His fate is sealed and I'm done listening, I want to play.

"See that's where you're wrong, I employ them, I pay them so they work for me and they do as I tell them to, not you." I turn to face him, as he is only standing at the side of me, the guard is holding on tightly to him.

I tell both of the men holding him to go and secure him to the wall, I want this over with now. I see them drag him kicking and screaming towards the bare wall with the chains hanging down from the ceiling, I know when I hear the clunk of the clasps that he is secure against the wall. His pleading comes back with full force as he begs and cries for me not to do this to him. I find it soothing when I hear someone's distress and their pain, it excites me on a deeper level. It's not the adrenaline that does it to me, it's the pain they are going to suffer at my hands that turns me on. I thrive on the pain I'm going to give.

I get my pleasure from their pain and I can feel the burn in my gut start, knowing what will happen. I am definitely going to have to get some release tonight, killing him is only going to secure that fact for me that my balls will be drawn up tight and my cock hard as rock.

"I hope you're looking girls?" I question them as I slowly walk towards the wall where he is secured, my steps don't falter, as I get closer to him. His face pales when I stop in front of him.

I reach behind me and pull out my gun. It's already loaded and I make sure the safety is off before I aim it at his head. I can feel my cock start to stir.

"Do you have anything to say before I do put a hole in your head" I wait for his reply but it does not come all I can see, is a look of utter defeat on his face. He knows there is no way out of this so why delay it. I squeeze the trigger of my SIG Sauer P226 and wait for slight recoil from the gun. The shot is loud as the sound reverberates around the warehouse. I watch as his head jolts back and then whips forward with the force from the shot. His body goes lax in the restraints, and that's when I see the crimson river seeping onto the floor that lets me know that the bullet has hit its mark.

I can feel the adrenaline coursing through my body. My cock is aching as it's straining against my trousers wanting to find that much needed release. I turn to face the girls disregarding the body that limply hangs. I don't care that they can see it, in fact I want them to get their fill looking at the dead body of Darren. They need to realise I am in control of what happens.

Looking at the two girls, I see Faith, she has a huge smile on her face. I watch her as suddenly her face changes to that of utter shock, I can see the turmoil of her mind, why she so pleased her dad is dead. It has still not broken her spirit and now I want to make sure I destroy it. What I am going to do next is sure to.

My balls are almost painful, and I am craving the need to hurt, to get my kicks from sinking deep inside a screaming body that fights against your hold. I can't wait until tomorrow. I am going to have to act now. I see Cami still sat next to Faith tears streaming down her face and I know what I must do so I don't hesitate.

"Now that the show is over, I want you to look at me Faith, because what I am going to say - I need to look into your eyes, to see your reaction, I want to see you break."

She looks me straight in the eyes and I see the anger there again that spark of defiance that she so badly wants to follow.

This is going to please me no end.

"You want to know why Faith? She just nods her head at me, it's now or never.

"Because your Damien killed my brother for what he tried to do to you," I see her thinking for a moment searching for who my brother could be, I decide to help her along.

"Conner was my brother!" I said pointedly at her. "I am going to enjoy doing what my brother could not manage to do. Firstly I am going to destroy something you love so that she will be no use to anyone ever again."

She quickly looks at Cami and tries to get up but the guards hold her still.

I grip hold of Camilla and pull her up by the arm her strength in her legs has not returned after being sat in the same position for so long. She tries to fight my hold as I drag her towards the back of the warehouse.

Her screams only excite me more.

"That's it baby fight me, it only gets me more excited." My grip is firm as I make my way to the room I am going to use.

Chapter Nineteen

Faith

I WAKE UP alone wondering why Cami is not back yet. I didn't sleep at all, with everything that's going on, listening to her screams killed me. She still hasn't been brought back to the room that Jake is keeping us in.

I sit on the cold floor wondering what has happened to us over the last day. I still can't wrap my brain around the idea that Jake is Conner's brother. The moment he said it my blood ran cold, and that feeling of fear came back tenfold.

How did I miss it? There must have been signs. I think back to all my encounters with Jake and there seemed to be nothing that truly stood out to me.

The thought of what Jake had said to me and I quote "*That the next time you see me cum, it will be inside of you eradicating every trace of him from your body, I will fuck you on top of his cold dead body. There is nothing you can do about it."* It was those words that sent the chills up my spine that set the alarm bells ringing, he was not going to give me a choice. He was just the same as Conner except I feared he was worse.

I went through so much after what Conner tried to do to me, I withdrew into myself closed myself off to the outside world, I could not face the world for 6 months, I lived and breathed Cami's apartment, the only place I went was to the therapist. But what I felt for Damien never faltered. Even after I found out who he was and what he did, my feelings never really changed. Sure it felt wrong how people would see it, but not in my heart. I knew that I was in love with him and being here now trapped in this place, I pine for him even more, but not wanting Damien to come for me, I want him safe.

I hear the door open and I know they are bringing Cami back. What has that sick fucker Jake done to her? I huddle closer to the wall as the guards place Cami on the floor. A gasp escapes me when I finally get a good look at her, only it doesn't look like her. Her hair is matted with blood and one eye is swollen shut, her nose has been bleeding and there are finger marks and scratches all over her body. I feel the tears coming to my eyes and I am helpless to stop them.

I rush over to where she is passed out on the floor and the guard just looks at me and offers me a first aid kit.

"She was lucky she passed out, if she hadn't he wouldn't have stopped until she was dead." Did he really just say she was lucky, looking at any part of her broken body you can see she is anything but, blood covers her from head to toe, big purple welts colour her beautiful skin.

"If you call this lucky, I dread to think what is unlucky to you. Why the first aid kit?" I was getting snarky with my reply but I really didn't care anymore. Looking down at my best friend I couldn't help it. I should have made him take me not her. Nothing in this whole mess has anything to do with Cami. I'm here because of my dad and Damien, but Cami is only here because of me and look what has happened to her.

"To help get her cleaned up a little, that's all, look I am only hired help I don't work for the psycho, and if I thought for a minute he was going to do that to her I would have tried to stop him." I see the truth in his eyes and I take the kit from him just nodding at him, I remember it was Jake that dragged her away nobody else, how were they to know what he was going to do to her, even I did not think that at first. It wasn't until I heard her screams flooding down the hall to where I tried to sleep curled up on the floor. It was no use I couldn't get out to help her, so I had to lie there on the floor and listen to what that monster was doing to Cami. "Can I have a little water please, so I can clean her up a little."

The guard walks back into the room a moment later with warm water and a sponge so I can at least mop up some of the dried blood.

"Thank you," I say to him in the kindest voice I can muster in these awful circumstances. Now I am wondering if the guard is doing this because he cares or if Jake is still playing some twisted game, to make us think someone is going to help us.

Before going in for the kill, and it's that thought that has me not trusting him. He leaves the room and I hear the door lock into place as I kneel down at the side of Cami.

I dip the sponge back in the now red water and try to clean her as best as I can, she is still out cold and I am beginning to worry a little. There is a cut still open on her head and I tried to put her jeans back on to cover her a little, but I couldn't pull them fully up. It's then I notice the blood that is now staining the rug from where she is laying it pools between her legs and my heart breaks that little bit more to know that he has taken her body and her power, all so he could exert his will over her, and beat her into submission. I hope she fought till the very end. It makes bile rise in my throat knowing that sick fuckers, like this walk among us.

I spend the next few hours just stroking the top of her hair, I don't even think it's a soothing benefit for her I think it's more for me. I think about everything while I'm sat there waiting for Cami to come around.

I think of my dad and how I watched as he was killed, and I don't feel anything, not even sadness that my father is no longer alive, sure my mum will miss the clothes and the shopping trips but I am sure she will land on her feet she always did. No the only thing I feel is relief that he is gone and I won't have him trying to sell me or trade me for money and that all this will be over soon.

"Faith" I hear in a quiet voice

I look down and see that Cami has her eye open and is trying to look up at me.

"Ssh it's ok Cami don't try to speak I got you," I say as soothingly as I can. I can feel the tears build again and I know it's guilt that I am swamped with. I brought her into this when I called her from the hospital all those months ago because I was selfish and couldn't be on my own. I wanted someone to help me and guide me and look what that caused. We are now sat in a concrete room with a dirty rug on the floor and no furniture, I caused her this pain. Me. Some friend I am. It should be me not her, laying here on the ground used and beaten within an inch of their life, if I could give anything for it to be me and not her I would do it in an instant.

"It hurts Faith, it hurts so much please, make it stop." Her broken voice makes my heartbreak with her words. What can I do to help her? I have done everything I can do with what I have.

"Ssh I'm so sorry Cami go back to sleep I'm not leaving you." I tell her soothingly trying to keep her calm as I continue to stroke her hair as I feel her breathing even out again. At least she is at least able to sleep through some of this nightmare. I rest my head against the wall trying to get comfy. I won't let go of Cami, I will stroke her hair as long as she needs me. I know it's not the best thing I can do but right now in this room it's the only thing I can do.

I don't know how long passes before the door flies open and a very smug looking Jake steps inside the room.

"So now you have seen what I can do" he leers at me and I can feel the anger in me coming to the surface *keep calm, keep calm*, I repeat over and over again I must not react.

"I have seen, I do have eyes, and I can say I'm most definitely am not impressed." Oh why can I not keep my opinions to myself.

"I do like seeing that fire in your eyes Faith, I am going to enjoy breaking you so fucking much, and I will break you, something that my brother could not manage. Looking at her you see that I am a man of my word I follow through." His words fuel my hatred more I will not cower and shrink in front of this worthless piece of shit.

"I don't think you will be doing anything of the sort, I will bite it off before I let your dick and your filthy hands come anywhere near me." I spit the words out Cami still sleeps blissfully with her head resting on my lap.

"You think I am affected by words of a woman like you? The harder you fight me the more I enjoy it; look at her. She tried to fight me it only took few hours before she finally gave in. I got bored quickly so I was getting ready to finish and take her last breath when she passed out. That is the only reason she is still alive. Not that I had any mercy or a change of heart, I like to know that my victims see their fate coming with eyes wide open it makes it more enjoyable for me." I hate that his words wound me. I can see the hunger there in his eyes, he wants to break me and strip me down piece by piece but it does not coincide with his plans. Well not just yet anyway.

"You think I am scared of you? I'm not, I won't fight you if that's what gets you off, I will just lie there, I won't scream, I won't fight and I won't say no. Lets' see you enjoy it then, you never know your dick might just go soft with me being willing." I say with as much bravado in my voice as I could find but on the inside I was scared and torn and almost at breaking point, the only thing that is keeping me going is that he does not have Damien.

"We will see what you are like when the time comes and the time is drawing near. Damien is due in a few hours then my plan can really take shape." With his words he left the room leaving me to ponder what had just happened.

Cami tries to sit herself up and when I try to help her she pushes me away. I sit her up against the wall so she could lean back and use it to hold her up.

“I really don’t feel right Faith. I don’t know what it is, my ribs hurt from his punches my head hurts from being smashed against the wall and between my legs hurt where he... Well you know you… cleaned me.” She tries to look away to hide her embarrassment but she hasn’t even got the strength to do that.

“Hey Cami don’t be embarrassed in front of me you are my best friend, Damien will come I promise. He will get us out just hang on for me, don’t give up the fight Camilla, I will always need you. I need you to stay focused on freedom because it will come.”

I hear her intake of breath and looked across at the tears that were falling down her cheek. She looks a mess and I can’t stand to see her like this. I have tried to clean her up and dress some of the wounds, but the blood is still flowing, she needs to get to a hospital to get checked over and time to heal, without fear of it happening again.

My friend is broken I can see it and I don’t think I have the energy to save us both, but I will try my hardest for her, I will be strong, I will fight or I will die trying, I will not give up. He will not get to her again.

***

Jake

I had to walk out of that room, I could feel myself

losing the fight with her. She is strong I will give her that. The fight in her eyes is still as strong as it was when I took them.

I thought that telling her who I was and doing what I did to Cami would be enough to break her but no she still fights and I can't say that it doesn't keep me as hard as fucking stone, I could feel my balls tightening with her sparing with me. But then she had to go and spout about being willing and will not fight and she was right my dick did start to deflate, it would not be the same. So I left the room looking at her pitiful friend, who put up a good fight, that was until the end when she passed out so I never got my finale.

Once I kill Damien and break Faith, that's when I will finally be better than Conner. I will have had the one person he craved and could not stop talking about after all the girls we have done this to, he never kept tokens like I did sure, he took a few polaroid's but never to the extent I did, I would keep their hair and I had pictures, with all of their names and dates on the back. So that I will never forget each time or each one of them.

The time was drawing nearer and I was starting to get impatient, months of planning were at stake here. All he had to do was show up alone and unarmed. I knew that if Malc came then there would be a real fight and by god that man can fight, I have seen it on a few occasions he is fast and deadly. He never misses his target.

I have a man at the start of the road to the warehouse to make sure he is alone in the car I will search him when he gets here for communications. I can't wait to tell him who I am, and see the recognition in his eyes when he realises that he set all of this in motion.

When I found my brother I was gutted at how he had been killed, the way his body had been mutilated and the words carved into his chest. Even though we were always in competition, no one was allowed to hurt him but me. Even though I had not known him all my life I looked up to him, he taught me everything I know, so it was only right for me to want revenge for his death and by god I will have it. I can taste it as the time was draws nearer. The smell of blood and death lingers in the air, I will be happier when I know it's Damien's blood that lingers in the air.

I need to make sure my final plans fall into place. I can't risk anything going wrong I had the room all set up for him and the table where I would fuck her while he watched, I will get great satisfaction in watching whilst he is strung up, helpless, with his dick cut off knowing that the only fuck she would get before she died was me. That he would have to suffer watching her scream in pain while I used her body for my pleasure.

The wall where the shackles are waiting for him. Every act that he did to Conner I will do to him, on the table set up close to the wall. I have the biggest hard on at the thought of what will happen in this very room in a few short hours, I will not masturbate like a fucking teenager, over what I will get to do soon.

Of what, I will get to taste, with my own tongue.

Of what, I will get to watch, with my own eyes.

Of what, I will get to feel, with my own cock.

Of what, I will get to kill, with my own hands.

Chapter Twenty

Damien

YET AGAIN I find myself on the sofa in the living room with the bottle of Jack on the table, I must have passed out again. I haven't been able to sleep in the bed without her. I can't stand the thought of not having her in my arms. I had to drink myself unconscious, so that I could pass out without thoughts of what she could be going through invade my mind. I am trying but failing to hold it together, when everyone has turned in for the night I found the bottle of Jack and started drinking.

I rise off the couch and make my way to the bedroom, I need to shower and get ready, after all today is going to be one hell of a day, however it ends.

Stripping off I walk in to the ensuite bathroom and step into the shower. I rest my head against the wall, the hot spray beating down against my back. I just stand until I can't take any more.

I finally emerge from the bedroom dressed in black trousers and a blue shirt, I can't really be wearing combat gear that might just scream 'I know what you're up to'.

I see Malc and Anton in the kitchen as I make my way through to get some coffee. I'm going to need a hell of a lot of that before I leave.

My mother is reading the paper at the table and she glances my way. She seems to have aged about 20 years overnight. I can't imagine how she must feel right now, she really bonded with Faith and Cami. To know that it's my fault that she feels this way. That all her memories of Bella are being dragged to the surface… It's like a twist of the knife hat's been wedged in my heart since I found out Faith was gone

"Morning Damien." My mother says in a sombre tone. I know what that tone means she is prepared for what could happen today. She knows how this story goes and that sometimes, not everything goes to plan. She was married to my father long enough to know what happens in times like this, but she knows when to question me and when to hold her tongue.

"Mother." I know I should ask her how she's holding up. It's not that I don't care, I'm just trying to keep a handle on my emotions. It's hard enough as it is, not to shout and scream at everyone. I'm barely holding on, I just want to get on with it and go and get my girl.

"Are you ready for today?" Anton says to me. Am I ready? I don't think you can ever be ready when the stakes are so high. One wrong move could bring the house down.

"I'll be fine. What about you? Is everything in place?" I ask him wanting to take some of the heat away from me, I can feel everyone's eyes on me.

"Yes we have the SUV stocked. We'll follow you there at a distance so we can bide our time, then come in and get you. Just remember he has to think you're alone and unarmed. Take your phone and everything you would normally take with you, and let him take them from you. That way he won't think you've done any planning beforehand." I nod in agreement.

I just hope everything goes to plan.

"Right one hour then we move out. Did you get back up sorted? I don't really want to go in with just us. We don't know how many goons he will have with him, or what her dad will be up to. I don't trust that motherfucker."

"I have two men joining us, they should be arriving at the house anytime now." He said as he glancing down at his watch.

"I take it they can be trusted?"

"Of course they can, I handpicked these two myself they are ex-Special Forces, so these boys know exactly what they are doing."

"Ok." As I leave the kitchen I wonder back down the hall to my office, I need to do something, to take my mind off what's going to happen next.

***

The drive to the warehouse is lonely and long, my heart is in my stomach the whole time. They follow behind me even though I can't see them, I know they're there. Watching, waiting for the right time to strike.

I have the case of money with me, it's beside me on the front seat and I realise I have to play this just right or else, I risk blowing this whole plan. I need him to think he is in control of everything.

It still gets to me that the piece of shit is in my building, talk about rubbing salt in a wound. This is going to end today, I will make sure of it. I just need Jake to believe that I know nothing and take me inside. That way I can make sure she is ok before the guys arrive.

I finally turn down the dirt road that leads to the warehouse; the car must find every pothole leading down towards the little car park at the side of the building.

Pulling the car to a stop, I don't see anyone around. I'm on edge, the hair on my neck standing on end in anticipating what is going to happen.

I turn off the engine and step out of the car, grabbing the case as I open the door. I look around and walk towards the doors, I still can't see anyone around. I'm at a loss but if Anthon said they're here. Then this is where they will be. I pull open the door and step inside the building, the door slams shut behind me.

As I walk further inside, the smell of death is in the air and I pull my hand up to cover my nose from the smell. I see the empty warehouse devoid of anything other than white painted brick walls the drying blood stains on the wall and floor, I wince inwardly wondering whose blood it is.

My heart races faster as I walk further into the room and then it shatters at the sight before me. Faith is bound and gagged kneeling in the middle of the room with her head downcast. I look at her and I want to run to her. Scoop her up into my arms and carry her away from all of this, but out of the corner of my eye I spot someone hiding in the shadows. Waiting for me to make a wrong move. So I do the next best thing I can do to give her a little reassurance that I am here, and that I have come to get her out.

“Faith, baby. Look at me” I say and I wait in silence listening to the wild thumping of my heart, hoping that she is not too traumatized.

They say everybody reacts differently to traumatic events, some people will have physical symptoms as well as emotional, or some will just have the emotional ones. I don’t care what coping methods she has because I will not give up on her. I will fight till the end to bring her back to me. I will repair her fragile mind, heal her broken body, and cherish her beautiful soul. I just want her to be here with me, in this room understanding what’s going on right now, so that she knows that I am here with her until this is over.

Her head slowly rises when she registers the sound of my voice. I can feel my mouth go dry and the hairs on the back of my neck stand on end.

Her emerald green eyes lock with mine and it takes me an age to recover from the vision before me. Dried blood is smeared across her perfect face, the dark circles under her eyes and the dry blood mattes her hair. I feel my anger rise at the vision before me, but as I look deeper into her eyes, I notice that she’s not broken, I see the determination and restrained anger burning in her eyes. I walk a little closer to her slowly not wanting to cause any extra problems. My strides are slow and cautious, I feel bare not having any weapon on me, but I can’t risk it, not where she is concerned.

“That’s far enough Damien” I hear Jakes voice and my blood boils. I turn slowly to face him.

“Hello Jake, I was beginning to wonder where you were.” He steps out of the shadows and stands behind Faith. I see the gun tucked into its holster and the glint of the knife sheathed in his belt.

"Well now, what is it that you think you know Damien that I am behind this whole problem? You caused this, not me."

"All I know is that you are here and I can't see Darren anywhere."

"Oh that's right, no you won't see him now. I shot him right in front of her and you know something? She didn't even blink as the shot rang out and his blood splattered across the floor."

I whip my eyes back to my girl and she nods her head at me to confirm what he is saying is truth and my heart sinks.

"So what do you want Jake? If you killed Darren then there must be something that you want?" I already know before he speaks that he is out for blood and revenge. I can see it in his eyes, in the way his body is hard and on edge ready to fight. There will be no reasoning with him. The madness takes over that feeling of compulsion and drives you to finish what you have started.

"Oh I know what I want and it's you dead. But first I am going to take the one thing you love most in this world and break it. Believe me when I say, I will break her, then I will take pleasure in knowing it will break you watching her. The last thing you will hear while you are breathing is her screams filling the air, as I fill her body."

I go to move but I am grabbed by both arms and dragged towards the back wall where I saw chains hanging. Now I know their purpose. He knows it's the only thing that might stop me getting to Faith.

"You're going to have to give me more than that Jake who is your brother?" He looks at me as if I have just punched him, like I should know who he is. I hear the clink off the lock as my arms are chained above my head making sure I can't escape.

"Conner was my brother and you killed him because of that slut."

"That rapist scumbag deserved what he got, I don't regret it and I would gladly do it again. It's one less sick fuck walking the streets of this city, I would say I performed a service, don't you think?" I see his face go red at my words, his hand curls into a fist. I see it coming as his fist connects with my jaw and I taste the tang of metal in my mouth and I chuckle a little.

"Feel better now do we?" I say to him knowing that I'm winding him up but wanting to keep the attention on me. I know Anton & Malc will be here soon.

"You know, when I found out what you had done, I knew that I wanted to kill you. I just had to find my way in and I did. It was almost too easy, so when I came in and offered Darren a way out, protection, he didn't care what I wanted. He was my puppet, all I had to do was pull the strings."

I need to goad him more he is still too calm and the ball is in his court. I need to change that

"So you had to go through someone else, to get to me because what? You're not man enough to come right out and face me? No you had to be a snake and slither back and forward between everybody. Like the coward that you really are."

"Oh I planned this to perfection, down to every last detail. Don't you worry it will be over soon enough, well for you anyway. I will make her suffer. I finally know how to break her. Knowing you will watch as I take her.

He starts walking back towards where she is still

kneeling on the floor. She doesn't make a sound nothing, not even when he pulls her up by the hair, removes her gag and slams his dirty mouth hard against hers, I watch in horror as his grip on her hair gets tighter, he snaps her head back hard thrusting his tongue inside her mouth.

Chapter Twenty-One

Malc

I WATCH AS he drives down that path towards the warehouse. We're blind as to what is going on. I could feel the anger swimming through my veins, not only did this *zalupa* have my best friend walking in there alone and unarmed, but he had my girl too. I know Damien can look after himself but I am itching for this fight.

The thought of him touching Camilla. It fucks me up. There is just something about her that gets to me on a deeper level. I don't want to fuck her and be done, I want to get to know her but she won't even entertain the thought. You can see how much she hates this world and I can't say I blame her, but this is all I know and it's all I will ever know.

My dad is standing by my side, we are beside the two SUV's with the guys my dad bought in to help us. I've never seen Damien this unhinged. I don't begrudge him happiness, God only knows he deserves it after everything that has happened with his sister and his father. He changed after that, became more cold and distant. Until Faith. She seemed to be able to get through to that heart of stone, even though nobody else could.

As we wait, I check my gun and check it again. I'm going to need to get through this. Who knows what is waiting for us in there.

We have gone over everything that we need to do, all we can do now is wait to make our move. Jake won't have a clue what has hit him. He won't walk away from this, I'll make sure of it.

"Right boys it's time to roll out." I hear my dad's voice. About fucking time! We head down the path, we can't drive down, they'd hear the engines and we want the element of surprise to last as long as we can.

The walk down the path is quick, I keep my eyes peeled and my gun raised scanning to see if anyone is around. The warehouse comes up quickly in front of us and I don't see anyone outside. I share a look with my dad and he takes one guy with him to scope out the outside of the building. I take the other man with me so we can make our way inside as quickly as possible. I quietly open the door and step inside the warehouse and I see the events unfolding before my eyes I am under strict orders not to kill Jake, Damien wants that pleasure, but what I'm seeing right now would give me just cause to do it.

Damien is chained to the wall but he is fighting against the restraints. Jake has his mouth on Faith and I balk at the sight, his grip is strong on her head but she is not crying, not fighting. I guess she's learnt as much about him as we have, just the thought makes my blood run cold. I don't see Camilla in this room. You would think that I would breathe a little easier but I don't, my heart speeds up because I don't know what has happened to her or where she is.

There are two guards are on either side of the wall where Damien is being held. I look to my dad wondering how we are going to do this and he just nods at me and with that one look I know it's show time, I make sure the safety is switched off and I get ready to do my thing.

Chapter Twenty-Two

Damien

I WATCH WITH a satisfied smile on my face, as I hear gunfire. My back up has arrived, thank god. I need to get out of these restraints. Now.

I see Jake quickly drop Faith to the floor. Like she's on fire. He whips himself around to see what the hell is going on. His face falls when he sees Malc and Anton and the two men that flank them both. The plan to get in unnoticed seems to have worked.

The first of Jake's men drops down at the side of me, the thud as he falls back and slides down the wall makes me grin. He might have just been a paid hand, but he kept Faith from me.

My breathing hitches when I see Faith trying to scuttle across the floor to avoid the conflict that's all around her. "Faith, move over to the wall" I scream at her, trying to be heard above all the noise and commotion.

For what seems like forever she doesn't move, so I scream at her again. Anger swells inside of me, I pull harder at the restraints that have me bound, the frustration I feel at trying my fucking hardest to break free is making me lose my shit. I need to get to her, told her I would never let her be hurt again and within a few days I have failed her.

"Malc get me out of these now." I bellow across the room at him he just looks at me, and gives me a look like I'm crazy. I know there's fucking bullets flying but I need out of here. NOW. I want to get to Faith.

Faith finally moves slowly across the floor on her hands and knees letting off little screams, when the bullets whistle past her. Jake catches her movement and quickly ducks down, he manages to get hold of her leg, as she tries to move towards the wall. She kicks out at him, trying to break his hold on her leg with no use. I try to pull harder, but I feel the burn in my shoulders when I pull. Watching in horror as he manages to get a tighter grip, pulling himself closer to her. I scan the room looking for Anton or Malc, anyone that might be able to get to Faith. "Malc, Anton….get Faith." I shout, but it's no use they are currently stuck behind one of the huge support pillars taking cover. All I want to do is get to free and to save my girl. I don't care about the bullets that are flying around. I would take a bullet for her, hell I would die for her if it meant she was safe.

The only other time I have ever felt this powerless, was when Bella went missing and I was away in another country. What could I do, at least I managed to get on the next flight home, when I found out what had happened. Then when I did get home, everything became clear and I finally figured out what he had done to Bella, I saw red, and finally took the action that would be needed against my father, the consequences that set my path in motion.

The day I saw my sister die in that room, her body lifeless on top of that bed, that is what broke me, that day I lost the first piece of my soul.

All I know is that all the light inside of me, all the good that my mother had made sure I had, left me that day. I didn't catch a glimpse of good again until I found Faith.

But even that doesn't compare with what I am going through right now. It's like watching everything play out in slow motion and there is fuck all I can do.

I pull even harder than I did before, I want out, I don't care about the burning or the biting, I can feel the warm liquid trickle out of the sores on my wrist.

The gunfire is deafening in the empty room. Faith's screams are cut through the noise, I can hear them all the way over here. Jake manhandles her up and grips both of her arms and shakes her. I am going to tear him limb from limb when someone gets me out of these fucking restraints.

Malc has managed to kill the guy that was firing at him, so that leaves one other and Jake. The two men that are dead have left nice pools of blood around them from their fatal wounds.

The gunfire stops and for a second I think it's over until I see Anton point the gun and pull the trigger, henchman number three slumps forward and that's him taken care of. There is only Jake left and he is mine.

"I see you still need a hand." Anton says to me.

"You might need these." Malc says to Anton, and I hear the jingle of the keys being tossed through the air towards Anton's head. I want these chains off me now; the thirst for Jakes blood is riding me hard.

"Get me out of these now!" I am demand "Where the fuck is Faith?" I yell as I see Malc over the other side of the room landing punch after punch to Jake's face.

I finally see Faith sat with her back against the wall, she is hugging her knees to her chest tightly. It just reminds me of the first time I came into that room, and saw her against the wall she looks pissed off. I can see her body shaking from all the way over here. Anton needs to get these damn things off me right now. I want my girl, I need to feel her in my arms..

"Hurry up Anton get me out of these damn things," I feel the tugging and pulling as the key is turned to undo the lock. The burning in my wrists increases, as they are released when the air hits the open wounds.

My arms drop to my sides limply, after being chained up for so long they feel numb.

I rush over to the wall and drop to my knees in front of her. Gently placing my hands on her face, I pull her to look up at me. I need to see them beautiful emerald eyes need them to keep me grounded.

I place my lips gently to her lips and I kiss her with all the tenderness I can muster considering I have not set eyes on her for what seems like days. All I really want to do is wrap her in my arms, take her to bed, and show her that he's mine. I release her lips and she lets out a little giggle. Even with all this shit she still blows me away. I stand up and pull her as close to me as humanly possible.

"I knew you would come, I never lost hope that you would come for me." Her faith in me blows me away. I would go to the end of the earth for this woman.

“Always baby.”

“I need to go and deal with Jake. Are you ok to wait here or do you want me to put you in the car?” Her face sets in a hard line at the mention of his name and I can still see the dried blood and dirt on her face and hair, and it breaks my heart to know that someone could do this to her.

“I want to be in there with you, I want to see you finish him Damien.” Her words send me in to a tail spin. She can’t see what I am going to do to him, what if she can’t accept my monster?

“No Faith you can’t be in there when I’m dealing with business I won’t allow it.” I try to keep my words firm, but she has that look that says I’m not going to win. I know that she has been through hell but looking at her right now, all I can see is a strong, determined woman who has a score to settle.

“You will not take this away from me Damien. That scum damaged my best friend, threatened the man I love, and killed my father whilst I watched and then to top it off he ejaculated on my face, so no Damien, I will be in that room while you kill him and I will enjoy every fucking minute of it.”

I fucking knew the *zalupa* would try something and to do that on her face is lower than low.

“What do you mean damaged your best friend? Where is Camilla, Faith?” I see my girl whip her head around to face Malc, a look of despair flashes across her face.

“Malc she’s in that room through there where they had us held, but I will warn you now. You will not like what you see. She needs to get to a hospital asap.” I don’t hear his reply as he turns to run down the hall, to get Cami.

It's just the two of us left standing in the room. I wrap her in my arms and take this moment to enjoy the fact that I have her back in one piece. A loud male scream has me letting go of Faith, and running down the hall, I stop when I find Malc on his knees with Cami cradled into him, rocking forwards and backwards. He is crying into her hair, whispering to her.

She is absolutely filthy and has blood all over her from her busted up face, right down to her bare legs.

"I need to get her out of her Damien, please I need to help her." He sounds broken and it pains me to see him this way, he has always been the strong and stoic one.

"Go Malc, get her seen to and we will join you shortly, when we have tied up these few loose ends."

He nods at me, scoops Cami up into his arms and stands to leave the room. I am sure Anton and I can handle Jake. He is shackled to the wall where I was and I can't wait until I get into that room with him. I will kill him, and I'll enjoy it. I don't take kindly to people trying to hurt what's mine.

"We have to deal with Jake now, are you sure you can handle this? This isn't going to be a fair fight, and he won't be walking away from this Faith. This shit changes you."

"I can deal with it Damien, after everything he has done to us, to me, I want him dead as much as you do."

Her words should surprise me but they don't, I know how strong she is and I've learnt what she is capable of doing. She is strong and caring and I am more in love with her right at this very moment than I think I have ever been. What kind of woman goes through what she has and still comes out fighting on the other side? That is the kind of woman I need with me for the rest of my life, to love, to honour and fucking cherish. I grab hold of her arm and slowly pull her towards where Anton has Jake held.

The main room of the warehouse is nothing special,

I see his body shackled up, and I won't say that a sick smile doesn't grace my lips at the smug satisfaction I get in seeing this.

"So what do we have here?" I say to Anton who is standing just off to the side of Jake. I really want to take my time, drawing every drop of blood from his body. Watching as the light fades from his eyes. I go to the bag that Anton brought, knowing what is inside this bag, it's like waiting for the presents on Christmas day. The tools that he uses to implement his punishments are legendary around our table, if a man knew Anton was coming for them, then you knew you would not be going out without a bang, that's for sure.

"So Jake, what should I do to you first?" I ask in an amused voice. "You understand why we won't be letting you get away with what you have done, don't you?" he doesn't even acknowledge me.

"First you infiltrated my family for your own advantage, then you work with her father to draw him further into this whole mess. Then you have the cheek to bring my girl to my warehouse and abuse her and her best friend." I am itching to get to work. I glance over at Faith as she watches on, making sure she is ok. I look back to the bag on the floor and reach inside, pulling out the first tool. I don't want to make it quick, I want to make him suffer like he has made them suffer. The silver blade catches the light as I pull it from the bag, I hear his breath hitch a tiny little bit when he sees it. I have the full use of my arms back now that all the blood has returned to them. The pins and needles have dissipated leaving me with just a dull ache in my shoulders.

I can see him now trying to fight against the binds. I twirl the blade around in my hand and through my fingers.

I press the blade into his cheek and slowly drag it down towards the corner of his mouth, I press the blade to the other side and repeat the process

"See, you don't understand how much I love that girl, with every fibre of my being I will protect her, I will always save her from fuckers like you and your brother. Of course we know who you are, those little tokens that you kept at your flat. Destroyed. Everything about you will be destroyed just like your brother was, and I will enjoy every second of it."

Chapter Twenty-Three

Faith

I AM IN this warehouse watching the man that I love, slice open another mans' face. If you would have asked me a year ago if I would have been standing here like this now, I would have said you were crazy. The good little girl like me would not deal with any sort of violence but after what I have been through these past few months has taught me one thing that even if you are good, the evil in the world will always find you.

I stand and watch every little thing, noticing the way Damien's skilled hands easily slice through his skin, I have never taken much notice of the way a man can hurt another man so easily, without regard for the person or their own humanity. He is like a man possessed while he gets to work. I watch on with a satisfied smile at the thought of this man getting what he deserves.

I have never been so excited to see Damien in all my life as I was earlier, but when Jake had me watch, as Damien was chained up to that wall it broke my heart. I think my mind just shut down. The man I knew who had come to rescue me was being led away where he would be unable to get free and help, I went numb just praying for the end, that it would be over quickly.

Then the gunfire started, and everything seemed to happen so quickly. The next thing I knew, I felt his warm lips against mine. I could not help the little giggle that escaped from my lips it was surreal, one minute I had resigned myself to my fate, then the next Jake was being dragged to the wall and Damien had me in his arms.

I knew with every piece of me that I wanted to watch as Jake took his final breath. To rid the world of these two sick bastards is a blessing and I will not think any less of my man for doing it. If anything knowing that my man will kill to protect me, only makes me love him more.

The loud crunch of bone breaking is a sound I will never forget, the garden secateurs in Damien's hands that he is using, to grip hold of each one of his fingers and cut them off just before each knuckle. His screams fill the space, but they don't bother me. So far three fingers are lying useless on the floor.

As he grips hold of each finger he says the same line to him, and it sends chills down my spine.

"You. Do. Not. Touch. What. Is. Not. Yours." He punches out every last word his accent fading more with each pronunciation. I hear the repeat of the crunch of bone and the screams and the dull thud of another finger hitting the floor. I am not sure how long the whole process takes, to rid him of all of his fingers. I think I stopped listening after five, just staring blankly looking like I am watching. Every now and then Damien will look at me with concern in his eyes, I am sure it was because I was watching this unfold.

The dried blood on my face is driving me crazy and I still want to wash his dirty seed off me, because all I could manage to do was wipe it, not scrub it clean. So what I am going to do later is get under the shower spray and remove every last trace of this hell away, but first I have to get through this.

The only thing I have to be thankful to Jake for is killing my Father. I can't say I was happy to watch that, but I am glad he is dead. I really am. The relief I feel now he's gone is immense. Now all the pieces of the puzzle have finally been slotted into place nobody sets my life now but me, I choose what I get to do, and whom I get to be with. Me.

Anton and Damien are both stood talking, I presume it is to decide what they are going to do next, before I think about it and stop myself, I have to get my say in. I don't care if they ignore me, I want Jake to know that I have a say in how this will play out.

"Strip him down Damien, I don't want any part of his body left unmarked. He deserves to bleed for what he has done to Cami and me, but also for every other girl he has ever laid a hand on."

"I think that's a great idea, babe, where shall we start?" I watch as he puts the secateurs down and picks up the knife again. Making his way back over to Jake he puts the blade under his top and quickly slashes the blade upwards so that it cuts his t-shirt off, then he pulls the trousers forward and slips the blade and cuts down each leg so that they fall in tatters to the ground.

He is now as naked as the day he was born, and I am glad to say that this disgrace of a human will not be gracing the earth much longer. Every time he breathes the same air as any decent person, it makes me sick. To think that he gets off on what he does to people, the lies and manipulation the web he has weaved for his own self-gratification.

The time has come for him to meet his fate

***

Damien

To hear her say what she wanted me to do to him, I forget for a minute that this is about Faith and what she has been through. All I want to do is kill him, as slowly and painfully as possible. It has set me alight with a new sense of purpose. I will make sure that he suffers, but to how she wants him to suffer… it does indescribable things to me.

"Where do you want him to bleed first, Faith?" I ask her hoping that she is strong enough to tell me exactly what she wants me to do.

"I want you to slice into his worthless excuse of a cock Damien. I want him to bleed all over the floor, while you slice in to every spare inch of his skin." Wow. She is gaining more strength every day. She is not letting what has happened to her define her anymore, she is grabbing life by the horns and giving as good as she gets. That's my girl.

I still have the knife in my hand from slicing his clothes off him, so to do what she has told me to do will be easy. The thought should bother me slicing into a man's balls, but this is not a man of consequence. Hell he won't be alive much longer anyway. By the time I am through with him he will be begging for me to end it all, I won't though. He can bleed to death slowly like his brother did.

"For you babe, I will do anything." I say to her as I step closer to him and see the disgusting sack that he emptied inside of all those defenceless girls, so I slice the knife down his chest to his cock and through his sack. It's like slicing through butter, the blade cuts through the skin with ease. I use light sweeps of the blade, not enough to kill instantly, but enough so that he remains on the brink his fingers have gone, his balls cut open and now, I am going to enjoy marring every last inch of his skin. I work quickly and skilfully using different strokes, some long and deep then short and shallow. I leave the rest of his torso until right at the end. I am going to enjoy carving into it. I'm going to make him scream.

"Anton, I am going to need the other knife." I ask him, I don't need to look at him to know that he will get it. I keep looking at this piece of shit, so far he has only screamed when I cut off his fingers and nothing since. I'm going to have to fix that.

"Here you go boss." I hear Anton say as I turn towards him. The blade is not that long but it is thick and serrated, this is going to hurt him when I use it.

"You're going to be branded now Jake, just like your brother was, he thought he could touch what was mine, he thought he could just take. When will sick fucks like you understand that no means no." I punch these words out, as I press the knife into his belly, I don't have to push too hard to hear him scream, the serrated edge of the blade is doing that for me.

I drag the blade up and down his skin, the screams are music to my ears. I hear a gasp somewhere in the fog that is my mind. I don't stop I carry on, needing to finish this so I can work on the next part of making him unrecognizable.

"Damien, you need to finish him." I here Anton say. I just grunt, not wanting to stop what I am doing, my girl needs to know that if anyone ever comes after her, I won't hesitate to destroy them.

The haze clears a little from my mind and I see that I have really done a number on his stomach and chest the words *'Rapist* bastard' are carved into his skin.

"Enough, Damien please." I hear Faith's voice and I get the feeling that I have let too much of my monster show. The ruthless bastard doesn't come out to often, but when it does, it's hard to get him under control.

"Tell me what you need Faith?" I ask her, I don't think I can go easy on him after what he has caused.

"I want you to finish this now Damien, and then I want you to take me home." I know that I will do what she asks of me. As much as I want to draw the pain out, and make him suffer as much as humanely possible, before he takes his last breath, if she wants me to kill him now I will.

"Jake, you know that I want to draw this out, and believe me when I say that I am going to kill you quickly because Faith wants me to. I think you now realise that I will do whatever for her, so I am going to give you this one chance to speak your last words before you meet your maker." His eyes have all but glazed over at my words, he is in that state where he has resided himself to his fate, he knows it's coming.

"Fuck you, you think I give a shit about dying, the only regret I have is not killing you and fucking her and then killing her too…" I punch him in the face at his last statement, the anger in me reaching boiling point. Blood is now pouring from his mouth, a few teeth have fallen out from the force of the blow. I take the gun from Anton, and point it straight at his dick, I will make it quick, but first I want that appendage gone, so that his last thought as I pull the trigger is, he just blew my cock off. Chuckling to myself, I fire quickly and the bellow of agony that resonates around the room makes me smile at what I see before me. The hole where his penis and balls used to be is a welcome sight, knowing that he will be done soon.

I lift the gun pointing the barrel straight at his head and squeeze the trigger. His head whips back with the pressure of the bullet being fired so close, right into the front of his skull. No one is living after that shot, I don't even need to check. I drop the gun and turn around to face Faith.

I don't have time to take a minute before she is running full speed into my arms. I wrap my arms around her and pull her close to me, she does not care that I am filthy, covered in the blood of the man I have just killed. She needs me.

I feel her squeeze me tighter, her arms clinging to me around my neck, it is then I hear her cries and my body automatically want's to sooth her and take away the pain.

"Ssh baby, I got you it's all over, I swear it's over no one will ever hurt you again." Lifting her up and she wraps her legs around my waist, her arms still clinging to me tightly. I carry her towards the exit of the warehouse, wanting to get her out of this hellhole.

"Burn it down Anton, I never want to step foot inside this place again."

The light is bright as I step outside the sun sitting high not often do we get such a bright day in London, my only hope is that it's a new start. I carry her towards the waiting car. I place her in the back, and get in beside her not wanting to be apart from her. I pull her back on to my lap and hold her close.

We set off and drive towards the hospital, where I can get her checked out, make sure she is really ok and not just putting on a brave face. She never has to pretend when I am around, if she is in pain or suffering I want to know, just like when she is happy and full of joy, seeing her beautiful smile is enough for me to die a happy man.

***

The sterile feel to the hospital room that Faith has been put in is cold and clinical, I hate it, I just want to get out of here and take my girl home let her rest, I want to be the only one to take care of her.

I sit in the waiting room, while the doctor is examining her. I was not happy about leaving her there while a doctor checked her out, but Faith demanded I go saying that she did not want me there while they checked her over. I can't even say it let alone think about it, Faith is adamant that he did not violate her, but they have to check apparently.

I look up to see Malc walking down the corridor towards the waiting room his face looks pained. I stand and make my way towards him.

"How's Cami, doing?" I ask him, his eyes showing his fear and worry.

"They said she has lost a lot of blood, and there is internal bleeding, they have taken her straight down to theatre." I have never heard him sound so defeated.

"She is in the best possible place Malc."

"What if she doesn't make it Damien? What will I do then? How will I."

I cut him off. Thinking like that isn't going to help anyone.

"She is strong Malc, she will be just fine, you will see."

Chapter Twenty-Four

Faith

I AM SAT on this damn hospital bed, waiting for the Doctor to say I can go. After all their checks apparently I'm ok just few cuts and scrapes, so I sent Damien home to get me some clean clothes.

He told Malc to keep an eye on me, but every time I ask him about Cami he clams up and turns away from me, so that he can hide the tears in his eyes, he thinks I don't see them but I do. The last time I asked him he stormed out of my room and slammed the door behind him as he left.

I also need to know where my best friend is and that she is ok, but he won't talk to me about her. I am sick of this waiting, I will bloody find out what's going on myself. I put my bare feet on the cold tiled floor of the hospital room and move to pull myself up, the bloody gown they have me in is open at the back and you can see everything, I move gingerly across to the chair, where I asked the nurse to bring me another gown and leave it for me. Spying the gown, I swoop it up and put it on like a robe so I'm covered on all sides.

I head to the door of my private room and pull it open, I wander down the hall trying to find the nurses station, I want to find out where they have Cami.

I go past a waiting room and pause for a minute, I notice a man sat in the corner with his head buried in his hands.

His head looks up sensing that he is being watched, it's then I notice that it is Malc and his cheeks are wet, I don't stop and think, I just rush over to him, I drop down to my knees in front of him.

Why won't anyone tell me what's going on, I need to know that Cami is ok. If anything has happened to her I will never forgive myself.

"Malc what's happened? Please just tell me. Oh god is she ok? Please let her be ok." I am begging on my knees, I don't care I just need him to tell me what happening. I don't care how stupid I must look here on the floor.

"They had to take her in to surgery Faith. The Doctor has just come out and explained to me what's going on." I pause for a second wondering why the Doctor told Malc.

"How come they told you Malc, and not her family or me?" I ask him.

"I said I was her husband, I couldn't bare not knowing. You and Damien weren't here yet. I didn't know her family, so I just said it was me." I can see the genuine concern for my best friend, I would have done the same if it were someone I cared about. It still does not tell me what the doctor has said to upset Malc.

"So what have they said?" As I ask he pulls me up from the floor and sits me in the chair at the side of him, he holds on to both of my hands. He gives them a little squeeze but it does nothing to reassure me.

"She had an internal bleed. That they had to fix, they said she had been kicked, punched and sliced with a knife, all over her body. They have also had to remove one of her fallopian tubes, and the chance of her conceiving is going to be harder now." I let the tears fall freely down my cheeks. I cry for Cami, I know how much she wants kids and she will be a great mum one day. Kind, caring and so loving, she would never hold a child back, will always put them before herself in everything she does. I just hope that she gets the chance to now. All this pain and drama has been caused by one mans greed, the ripple effect that it has had on my world has been catastrophic to say the least and I don't know how I will ever come to terms with what has happened over these last few months. The hurt and pain it has caused has burrowed deep inside of me.

I hope and pray that Cami can forgive me. I know she is alive and that is a huge relief. That girl has been my rock through all of this and I think it's time I became hers.

"When can we see her?" I ask him, not really expecting an answer as he has buried his face in his hands again. I just want to break the eerie silence, which hangs between us.

"She's still in recovery, then they are moving her to a ward. They said when they have her on a ward I could see her." I don't miss the way he shut me out and said I instead of us. I guess I deserve that. If I had never had the hospital ring her all those months ago, then she would not be here now. Going through major surgery and possibly losing her chance to have children. I stand to head back to my room, at least I know she will be ok.

"Thanks for telling me, I best get back to my room." I don't give him time to answer, as I practically turn and run back to my room.

I fall on to the bed and I start to cry, I let it all out. Everything that has happened has finally caught up with me and I feel like I am going to break. I feel I hand on my shoulder, as the tears consume me, my body shudders uncontrollably.

"I didn't mean to hurt you Faith, I understand you need to see her just as much as I do, if not more. I realised what I said, as soon as you left and the way it came across." The gruffness of his deep tone makes me realise who it is speaking. I did not expect Malc to have followed me, or give me any soothing words after everything, but I am glad all the same.

"Tell her I'm so sorry Malc, I didn't mean for any of this to happen to her. I love her so much I would never want her to be hurt." The tears have not stopped, I can feel myself heaving in-between sobs.

I feel him rub small circles on my shoulder trying to calm me, but it's not working. The only person I want to console me is Damien and he is not back yet. He needs to get me out of this place. I need to forget and the only person that can make that happen is Damien.

"I will tell her Faith, but you're going to have to give her time."

"Faith, what's wrong? Why are you crying?" I turn over in the bed to face the door where he is standing. He drops the bag and rushes over to me, Malc steps out of the way just in time to let Damien get to me. He scoops me up and holds me close, just letting me sob into his chest. The feel of his warm body against mine and his heart beating against my ear does calm me. I relay everything that has happened while Damien was away, Malc steps out, I don't think he can listen to me retell it, he is having a hard enough time living it.

"I need to shower and dress do you think you can help me please." I ask him, I hope he will say yes but I'm a mess, the dried blood all over me, the bruises and scratches that cover my body, I won't blame him if he won't.

"I can't Faith. If I see you in that shower things are going to lead somewhere that they can't go right now." I'm flooded with disappointment, I knew that all this crap would be too much for him. That he can't look at me or that he does not want me in the same way as he did before. I unravel myself from his arms and try to make my escape to the bathroom, but he snags hold of my wrist and turns me back to face him.

"You can get that thought out of your head Faith. I want you so much. I can see the cogs turning inside your head." He grabs hold of my chin and kisses me with a passion that I have not felt for days, his tongue tries to invade my mouth, to deepen the kiss and I allow it needing to feel that connection to him.

"The only reason I am not going in that bathroom with you is that I don't want to fuck you in some hospital bathroom. When I take you again it will be in our home do you understand me? I want to hear you scream my name as I take you." My mouth drops open at his statement as I wander into the bathroom to get myself clean, and ready so that I can go home and be with my man.

I step under the warm shower spray. I shiver at first it is hot enough to cleanse the dirt and the grime away from my body, as I contemplate the whirlwind that has been the last few months of my life.

On the outside looking in, a few months ago I had a father and a mother who appeared to love me, as happy without a care in the world. Then my life was turned upside down, all my plans were snatched from under me by my father of all people. How can a father, the one person in this whole world who is supposed to look out for his little girl make them disposable object?

The only thing that worked out for the better is Damien, who I love unconditionally. Regardless of his faults and his ideas of keeping me safe. He is the one person who I know will always keep me safe and come for me. No matter what happens, he will always be there for me.

I let the steam surround me in a cloud just wanting to hide for a little while, to be invisible wishing none of this has happened to me, but then I realise that if I did not go through hell I would not have Damien in my life. A knock on the door pulls me from my run away thoughts.

“Faith? Are you ok in there?” I hear the concern in his voice, and it touches my heart that after everything we have been through he still has this soft side that only I get to see.

“Just a minute, I’m just finishing up.” I say to him in hopes of soothing his concerns. I quickly wash myself, ignoring the pain that courses through all of my body. I shut off the water and step out and towel myself dry, realising my clothes are not in here shit, I need to go back out into the room and grab my bag. I pull open my door and step out, I watch as his eyes roam over my scantily clad body. I see the hunger in his eyes but I also see the anger at the marks covering my body.

"Sorry, I forgot to take my clothes in there with me let me just grab them, and go back to the bathroom." I feel dirty, I know my body does not look great but it feels a hell of a lot cleaner than it did.

"I am not angry at you Faith or repulsed the way you look. I am angry at what he did to you. I know that we have dealt with him but the feeling I have when I see you in pain or hurt makes me want to hurt him all over again."

I feel relief at his words and I drop the towel where I stand in front of him.

Chapter Twenty-Five

Faith

THE RIDE TO the house is quiet and all I want to do is sleep. I didn't see Cami before I left the hospital but Malc stayed behind. He refused to leave her there on her own. I think it's sweet. When the car comes to a stop outside of the house I open the door. I've missed this place. It's strange to think how much like home it has become.

I can see myself here for the rest of my life. Watching our children grow as I grow old with the man I love. Knowing that my life here in this world would not be complete without him.

I walk through the doors of the house and a wonderful smell hits me straight away drawing me towards the kitchen. I love the smell of roasting ham, I can almost taste the honey glaze coating. Wandering inside I take a seat at the table and I see Anton already sat there with Lily. A huge smile of relief crosses her face when she sees me.

I feel her arms circle around me, I feel the love emanate from her. The sheer feeling of joy runs through me at the thought of being truly accepted. I shut it down quickly. While I am here getting cuddles and sympathy, Cami is lying in a hospital bed recovering.

"I'm so glad you're home safe Faith, we were all so worried about you." My eyes start to fill up and I have to take a big deep breath to get myself under control.

"Thank you, I'm glad to be home." I say with true conviction in my voice, because I am glad it's over and I am glad I'm home.

I sit down and try to have a small plate of ham, egg and chips. There is something to be said for a simple meal. It soothes the soul and gives you comfort.

It's getting late and I have to be up early in the morning to go and visit Cami. I need to see her. If she won't see me then I will go back every day until she will. There is no way I am giving up on her, she would have never given up on me.

"I am off to bed everyone; I will see you all tomorrow." I stand to leave, hearing all the goodnights called to me as I make my way down the hall to the bedroom.

I open the bedroom door and the sight that greets me makes my cry instantly. I feel the heat at my back and I know who is behind me, his warm hands wrap around my waist and guide me into our bedroom, the white rose petals scattered on the bed, the candles that surround the bedroom, have my heart melting and my insides heating up.

He presses tender kisses to my neck, working his way down from my ear to over my collarbone, still clothed I can feel the heat of the kisses through the t-shirt, it's like he is kissing all the bad away.

Slowly I lift up my arms, as he takes the hem of my t-shirt and slips it over my head, my top half is now bare for him as he traces his lips down me, his kisses are like feathers across my skin making it tingle and burn for him all at the same time.

He unsnaps my jeans and gently pushes them over the swell of my hips and towards the ground. I lift up each foot one at a time to remove them, once they have gone I am now on show, every scrape, every bruise, I try to cover myself from his view, but he does not let me, he holds my arms gently to my sides as he continues to kiss me, even more seductively than before, I get so lost in the pleasure that he is bringing my body.

I don't even see him remove his clothes. He lifts me into his arms, and gently lays me down in the middle of the bed, my body is already on fire every nerve ending alight and craving his next touch. He is doing exactly what I need him to do he is changing the memory for me, washing away the bad, until I get the memory of just him and me. It doesn't block everything out, but it helps to heal the scars that have been left, forever imprinted in my mind. His eyes find mine through the passion, all I see is love shining back at me, it makes my heart burst even right now, in this moment he wants nothing but me and the love I can give him in return.

"I love you Faith so much, I could not live in a world where you do not keep me in the light."

I don't care that I have tears in my eyes this amazing man has just told me I am his world. Now is for the future not the past, for the living not the dead.

I open wider for him to nestle right where I want him, hoping that he understands that I need him now more than ever.

"I love you too Damien, more than you will ever know we may not have started right, but I will always be your light in the dark, the good to the evil that will never destroy us."

As I finish declaring my love, he presses himself into me, so slowly filling me with every inch, I feel myself stretch around him my hands find his back and I cling to him, to feel every ridge of his cock moving slowly in and out of me is ecstasy, a high that I never want to come down from, he meets my lips and takes my mouth, his tongue moves at the same agonizing pace as his hips do pushing himself deeper inside me filling me top to bottom, surrounding me with all of him I feel consumed. And I love every fucking minute of it.

"Come with me Faith, I want to finish with you." His words send me over the edge and I scream as my muscles tighten and I contract around him milking him for everything he has to give me. I feel him pulse deep inside of me, pausing when he can't go any further; his breathing has hitched a little.

"I want you with me always Faith, I never want to be without this feeling, you are mine. I never want to feel what we have just been through again, the thought of losing you killed me inside, I can't survive without you. Will marry me Faith?" I look at him, as I still feel him nestled deep inside waiting for my answer. I look into his eyes, did he really just ask me to marry him?

Do I want to marry him knowing how this relationship started, but looking up to the man I love knowing that he would die for me, has killed a man for me, but above all else he would change for me, it's not that I want him to change, the fact that If I did ask him he would and that's enough for me no longer will I ever feel unimportant, I will always be wanted and needed, to Damien I am his.

"Yes."

He kisses me and pulls out, pulling me onto his chest, I soon drift off knowing that I have found my place, as long as Damien is by my side I can take on the world.

Epilogue

Faith
Six months later

I CAN'T BELIEVE today has finally arrived. I stand in our bedroom with Cami and Lily, wearing my ivory corset and panties. The silk is so soft against my skin, it's like I'm wearing nothing.

My dress hangs on the rail inside the wardrobe, the strapless ivory silk mermaid style with the lace over dress, with fitted sleeves flows over the top of the gown like a glove, a perfect match all held together with the diamond belt. I still don't know how much the dress cost and if I asked, I probably wouldn't have bought it but as soon as I saw it while shopping with Cami, I knew it was the dress I would be saying “I do” in.

The journey to get us to this point has been hard and not without its trials, Damien asked me to marry him pretty much as soon as we got home from the hospital. I said Yes, but it would not be until everyone I loved could attend.

There was no way I was getting married without Cami there with me. Her journey has been worse than mine, she only left the hospital 8 weeks ago. At first she refused to see anyone, demanded that I go away, that I had caused all of her pain.

Damien made sure she got the best help, I kept going back and slowly as time went on she let me back in. That day was hard, I think we spent the 2 hour visiting session just crying and holding hands. I tried not to look at her differently but she was different. Gone was the girl that got me out of the apartment for a haircut and dinner.

The girl in her place was devoid of all feelings, she went through the motions of living; she slept, she ate, and she read but that was all she did. She is still dealing with what happened to her and the one person that seems to be able to get her to do anything would be Malc, he has been there every day even when she shouted and screamed at him; he never gave up, never lost his temper with her.

He was the one that finally told me to marry Damien, because I could be waiting forever for her to come back to me, to be the friend she was. So here I am, having my hair and make-up done, getting ready to walk down the aisle to my future.

“Faith, this belonged to my mother.” I look up and notice the beautiful blue hairpin, the little stone that is surrounded by two intertwined gold rings. “That’s stunning Lily.”

“The two gold rings represent you both and the blue gem is your marriage, it shows that as long as you are honest and love each other, the gem will stay intact but pull them apart you risk breaking it." Her voice is so gentle you could get lost in it forever.

"I want you to wear it today as you walk towards my son, it is your something old, something borrowed and something blue. And before you say no, this is a tradition all the women in our family have." My fingers tentatively reach out to take it from her but she bats my hand away and proceeds to put in to my hair, slotting it in at the veil that is sitting just under the bun in my hair.

They say that people who get married quickly go in blind, not knowing what each person is like. I know this man that I am walking towards inside out.

Malc is walking me down the aisle of our garden ceremony at the house, he promised to show me the garden at night with the twinkling lights, when he did I fell in love and I knew then that this would be where we would marry, under the stars. Why would I want to get married anywhere other than our secret garden? This is the first place I saw the sweeter side of Damien, the one only I see.

As I walk closer to Damien I get ready to meet him at the altar, Malc stops and turns me to face him, then leans in close to my ear.

"Never give up on him Faith, you're his whole world." As I turn back the tears fill my eyes, I give him a kiss on the cheek as he finally gives me away to Damien.

I gaze up at him so I can speak my written vows for him.

"I promise to always be your light, when you need to be shown the way.

I promise to always stay and fight, and never take flight.

I promise to love you until my dying day: to be by your side and show you a better way.

With my love, I am yours,"

I see the tear that falls down his face, he speaks his vows to me and I lose myself in his words.

"You're the good to my evil, the light to my dark, you brought me back and showed me the way. I thought I lost the man I was before but you saved me Faith and for that, I give you my heart, to keep with you. You're my forever Faith, ever thine, always mine."

We speak the rest of the vows together, the love, obey, honour and cherish till death us do part,

I hear the minister announce you may kiss the bride, it's official, I am now Damien's wife. He kisses me with such sweet passion, that of a man who cherishes his woman.

The rest of the evening passes in a blur and it's soon time for us to jet off on our honeymoon. All the bags are in the car waiting. All I have to do is throw my bouquet. I stand in front of the door to the house with my back facing everybody; I hear the cheers and whistles from all of the guests as I get myself ready to throw.

I close my eyes, grip my bouquet in both hands and throw my arms up to release it over my head. I spin around to see who has caught it and I smile so brightly when I see that it's Cami who has hold of it, though I can't say she looks best pleased.

As we prepare to leave, we say goodbye to all our guests and say our thanks to everyone for coming to make our night so special.

I take Cami to the side; tell her I love her and that I will see her soon. Pulling her into my arms I hug her giving her a kiss on the cheek, we are not back to where we used to be but for now we are whole in the only way we can be.

I slide into the back of the waiting limo, which is going to take us to the airport. I have been waiting all day to get to speak with him alone. I have been waiting since I had the scan the other day confirming my suspicions. I kept putting the weight gain down to comfort eating, the dress fitter was not best please having to keep altering my dress, but Damien had been away on business for a month. I pined for him, that feeling of being alone after everything that had happened, so I was eating more, well now I know why, I was eating for two.

I turn to face my husband whom I love with all of my heart, knowing that today is the start of our future, one where we plan the journey, no one else.

"Damien?" I ask using that tone, which tells him I want to talk.

"Yes, Mrs Volkov. I love you having my last name finally you're mine in body, soul and name now."

He places his lips against mine this time it's a kiss that sends a jolt of pleasure straight to my core, I open my mouth so that he can slip his tongue in, and deepen the kiss, I pull away knowing that I have to talk to him.

"Damien, I have to tell you something."

His lips never leave my neck or my collarbone he is nipping at the lace of my dress and it is driving me to distraction.

"Yes my love?" He says in that oh so sexy tone.

"You have me in one more way now, other than name." I say waiting for him to click, but it never happens.

"What way is that, *moya lyubov*." Oh god he is pulling out the Russian he is killing me slowly.

"We're going to have a baby." I just say it as quick as I can; it's not something we have really talked about before, so I'm not sure if this is a good or bad thing.

"I'm going to be a father? So the new curves I have been feeling is you carrying our child" I just nod not able to form words yet the look of sheer joy crosses his face.

"I love you Faith, I could not have asked for a better wedding gift, I have my wife and our child, you complete me Faith."

I start to cry I don't care if I get panda eyes on my wedding day, what I need is for my husband to take me into his arms and never let me go.

I have everything a girl could ever want a loving, sexy husband, a home, a family, and now our child growing in my tummy, ready for us to keep her safe.

I wonder if now is the time to tell him that it's a girl.

THE END

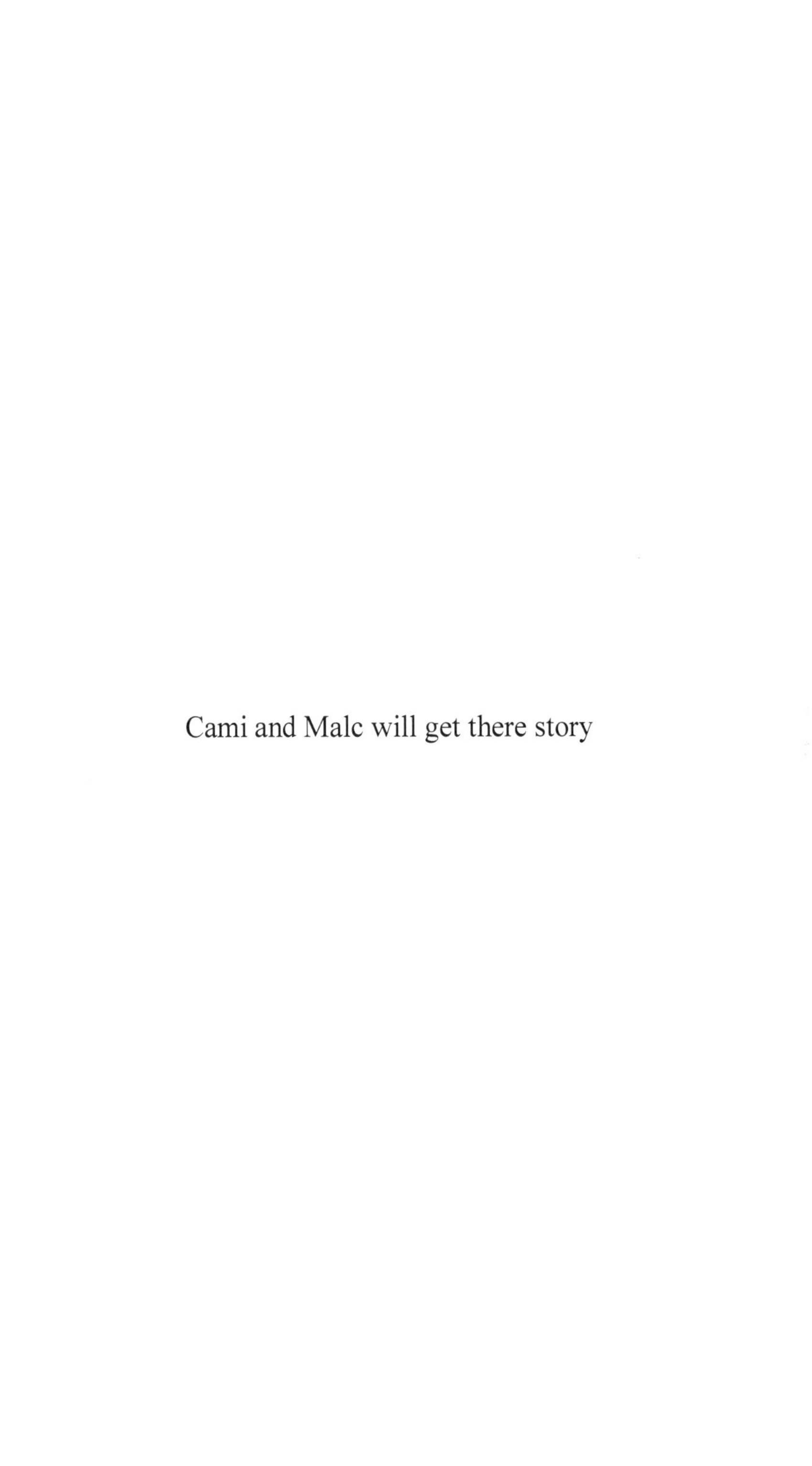
Cami and Malc will get there story

ACKNOWLEDGEMENTS

Thank you to my beta readers, Anne and Karen. Your thoughts and words have kept me grounded.

Thank you to Francessca Webster http://www.francesscas-romance-reviews.com for a beautiful cover and for organising my release. You are truly amazing.

Thank you to Sally Orchard and Elisia Goodman for editing and for all the support you have given.

Thank you to all the authors and friends who have supported me on this amazing journey.

Thank you to Muriel Garcia for your support and the formatting. It was very much appreciated.

And thank you to you, the reader, for buying this book.

Without your constant support we would not write. Your comments and reviews mean everything to us indie authors.

About The Author

I am a mum to six wonderful children, and married to an amazing man who supports my dream to write.

I wouldn't say that I wanted to be a writer from when I was little.

I only really started reading often when I had baby number five, as he was born very early and spent thirteen weeks in special care. It was then that I discovered my love for reading.

From then on, I was hooked. I read all types of romance books.

It dawned on me that I wanted to be more than a mum/reader/blogger. I wanted to write, as I have a very active imagination, so I put pen to paper.

I wrote my first book, *Obsession*, this year and I am super excited to say that it will be published on the 29/09/2015.

Coincidentally, this is my thirtieth birthday (at least I won't forget the day my first book went live).

I write romance - contemporary, dark and erotic.

I like to write about loss, pain and love, and what it's like to fight for your happy ever after.

Printed in Great Britain
by Amazon